They Never Really Leave

By
Stephen M. Braley

PublishAmerica
Baltimore

© 2010 by Stephen M. Braley.
All rights reserved. No part of this book may be reproduced, stored in a retrieval system or transmitted in any form or by any means without the prior written permission of the publishers, except by a reviewer who may quote brief passages in a review to be printed in a newspaper, magazine or journal.

First printing

All characters in this book are fictitious, and any resemblance to real persons, living or dead, is coincidental.

PublishAmerica has allowed this work to remain exactly as the author intended, verbatim, without editorial input.

Hardcover 978-1-4512-7523-0
Softcover 978-1-4512-7524-7
PUBLISHED BY PUBLISHAMERICA, LLLP
www.publishamerica.com
Baltimore

Printed in the United States of America

Dedicated to:

Aunt Rosi Cali for her copyediting and encouragement
Tim Bryant, friend, for always being there for me
James A. Kinney, Esq. for his wisdom and encouragement

To Mr. Gregory A. Freeman, whose outstanding book "Sailors to the End" was the impetus and inspiration for this novel.

Chapter 1

"This way, please." The hostess motioned onward to Jimmy Gallant, but her smile disappeared after he thanked her and she heard his northern accent. She led him to a nice spot on a corner of the deck with a great view of the beach and water. A tarnished brass oil lamp flickered on a tattered red and white checkered tablecloth before him. Slapping a sticky menu down before him, she monotoned, "Your waitress will be with you shortly," gave him a cursory smile and vanished. The place was a paradise for eccentric seafarers. A myriad of netting, shells, anchors, ships wheels, even a torn sail on a mast from a boat adorned the beachside entrance to the cafe. A large fiberglass swordfish swung aimlessly beneath the neon sign, its broken tailfin dangling by a remnant of a rusted length of chicken wire. A mangled crow's nest from a seafaring vessel arose from the center of the building, as if a young seafarer still stood watch in it for high seas, storms, or pirates. A wide sun-bleached deck jutted out on the upper level of tables overlooking the ocean, giving partial shade to a jumbling of small, tightly-placed round tables on the level beneath it. The sheer eccentricity of the disheveled heap of a tourist trap had intrigued him, that someone had actually taken the time to rescue all this sea-washed junk and had assembled it to create the old café.

The frantic servers vaulted from table to table and back to the kitchen and bar, servicing the demanding tourists. His mouth was so dry that his tongue stuck to the roof of his mouth. Someone could at least bring him a glass of water. The wait staff was a blur around him. He sat up straight at the table and unfolded the napkin, placing it on his lap. His stomach was aching for food. But one after another, the wait staff flew past his table, not even acknowledging him. "Uh, excuse me—" too late, that one was really fast. "I'm sorry, Miss"-nope, she got away too. The smell of seafood didn't appeal to him at all but he'd set his eyes on an eight-ounce sirloin steak on the menu. He'd now been there a full thirty minutes, and he saw people who'd arrived after him being served already. Jimmy Gallant, normally laid back and easy-going fellow was about to lose his cool when couldn't intercept a waiter or waitress for anything.

Tapping his foot to the sound of "Mack the Knife" that was playing on the jukebox, Jimmy Gallant was drumming on the tabletop as he waited and still tried to keep his temper in check. He leaned back on two legs of his chair absentmindedly. Aha! Was his luck changing? One of the waitresses paused at his table to double check her math on a dinner tab before she scooted away.

"You! Excuse me, but"-no, she was off again, without hearing a word. Losing his balance on the back two legs of the chair, he toppled over backwards. He kicked the table and knocked the oil lamp to the floor, spilling its contents that flamed up in a small blaze on the deck floor. A lady screamed "Fire! We're all going to die!" as Jim beat the flames with the tablecloth.

The minor combustion sent the panicked crowd into an alarmed frenzy pushing each other down the long deck stairs to the beach hurling obscenities at Jimmy. They shoved their way toward the exit, knocking trays and plates out of the hands of the wait staff. "Just hold it, everybody-keep yer shirts on, for crimony's sake." A tall redhead in a yellow polka-dot halter top and cut-off denim shorts aimed a fire extinguisher at the flames and quickly put it out. "All right, all right, now, y'all come on back up here. The catastrophe's over, come on, get up here now. Oh Lord, lady will you stop cryin'? Come on back to your seats. We got a crowd a mile long out back waiting for your tables. Y'all come on back up here and finish your meals, the show's over. See?" She waved her arm over the smoldering circle on the old wooden deck. "No more fire." Everyone glared at James as they took their seats again. "All right, all right, now, mind yer own business and eat, there's forty-five people standing out back in the heat waitin' for your tables."

The redhead whirled around to confront Jim. "Mister, just what in sam hell did you think you were doin'?"

Some man at a table to the right scowled at Jimmy and said, "Damned fool—my food got cold." The redhead towered over him, looking down over her ample bosoms barely contained by the halter top. Hands firmly planted on her hips, she demanded, "Well, what were you tryin' to do, burn this old dump down?" He leaned against the deck railing. He felt sick. He was hungry, angry and humiliated, but he managed to squeak out "I'm sorry" to the imposing amazon leering down at him. The words caught in his throat as he spoke.

"You're sorry. Well, what're you gonna do now, eat your dinner on your lap?" The acrid smell of the singed deck was slowly dissipating in the air.

"Dinner-what dinner. Can't even get a glass of water in this joint," Jimmy muttered. I've been waiting for over forty-five minutes and people who came after me are gettin' their food already."

She was unsympathetic. She rolled her eyes and demanded, "What are you, a sailor or a grunt?"

Seaman Gallant stuck out his proud chest. He answered, "A sailor, why?"

"'Cause nobody comes in here and makes this much trouble unless they're a sailor or a grunt." She leaned closer to whisper, "even the worst of these knuckle head tourist losers got more brains than your kind. Haven't you noticed the signs around town-dogs and sailors keep off the grass?" Despite her demeanor, Jimmy was struck by her beautiful ruby-red lips and her huge mane of scarlet red hair and her perfect figure, and wondered how such stinging words could come out of someone who looked like her.

"That's a really rotten thing to say," he protested.

She sighed. "Yeah, well, whatever. I gotta get back to work." She had his Irish temper up now and there was no turning back.

"Just a minute, miss. You know somethin'-you're about the rudest person I've ever met. I'd like to talk to the manager. What's your name, please?" His voice squeaked. He hated how his voice did that when he was really, really mad.

"Name's Mary. Mary Bauer. Now would you like me to take your order or just douse myself in kerosene so you can light a match?" The older couple at a table to his left laughed and the lady snorted, and for the first time, a thin, wry smile broke out across the redhead's sultry lips. She was obviously starting to enjoy this.

"Where-how am I supposed to eat like this?" The table teetered before him as he balanced it on three legs.

She stood up straight, order pad in hand as she swept her amazing long waves of scarlet hair back over her shoulder. "Well, Mr. 'Sailor boy,' I guess since you just ruined our only open table, you'll have to figure that one out on your own. Now do you wish to order now or not?"

"Just bring the manager to my table, please." She rolled her eyes and covered a yawn with her hand.

"Mister, you're looking at her."

Jimmy tried hard not to show his surprise. "Well-I'd like to see the owner, then."

"He's in the back tryin' keep up with these gluts's orders. He's the cook. You want his number, Admiral?" The young man stood and lowered the table onto its side.

"No, forget it. I'm gettin' out of here. This is the crummiest restaurant I've ever not eaten at." The feisty redhead feigned shock and loss and she covered her mouth with her fingers. She shouted after him. "Ah gee, mister. We sure hate to lose you as a customer. But I guess what we lose in your business we'll make up with our fire insurance premiums!" Spontaneous laughter and applause rustled through the crowded terrace, as though it was the evening's dinner show. As he left Jimmy wished he'd have steered clear of that joint.

His pride still massively wounded, the homesick sailor ambled along the beach, his soul as arid and parched as the sand he kicked up in front of him. He was hundreds of miles from home with no one that cared about him within close reach. He'd never felt so alone.

Dressed in his "civies," he looked like any other tourist on the beach. He was a handsome boy, sandy-blonde hair and azure blue eyes that melted you when they met yours. At 6'3", his 170 pounds were lean muscle, having been a swimmer and runner since he was fourteen. He had a trademark smile that might have been mistaken for a smirk; it was really just a slightly mischievous little half-smile, his lips pursed, one that he never did know how charming it was. As Jimmy walked further on down the shore, the red neon sign glowed in the seaside dusk and he could still make out the words "Chesapeake Crab House."

"Typical tourist trap," he grumbled. "Chesapeake Crabby House" should be it's name, he said out loud. The whole thing looked like it might have drifted ashore as rubble and assembled itself as such.

"Of all the dives in this town, I'd have to pick that one." Jimmy walked a little further up the beach and found a Howard Johnson's restaurant. What a relief.

That redhead—Mary—she was such a witch. But she was the most gorgeous witch he'd ever met. And the young seaman knew already that after he'd had time to settle down and lick his wounds, he'd be back to check her out again.

****

The next day, Jimmy bolted down the dock to the payphone and fumbled through the phone directory. "Chesapeake Crab House, 595-6011." He held his breath as he dialed. Busy. He slapped the receiver down and his change rattled out. He dialed again. 595-6011. Busy. "Darn it." He rammed the receiver into the cradle again. He drew a big breath and released it slowly. "Jerk-get a hold of yourself. You're totally nuts over a rude waitress who hates you. Who're you foolin'?" He dialed again anyway.

"Chesapeake Crab House."

"Uh-hello?"

"This is Chesapeake Crab House, how can I help you?" the voice sounded rushed and impatient.

"Yes, I'd like to know if… I mean, I'd like to make a reservation for tonight."

"What time and how many sir?"

"Seven p.m., I think, and just me."

The voice on the other end was impatient. "You're calling for a reservation for a party of one, and you think it will be for seven o'clock?"

"Yes, and could you please tell me—"

"Name, please."

"Gallant. Gallant's the name."

"Gallant?" The impatient man repeated, huffing a laugh.

"Yes, but…"

"That's a table for one at seven o'clock. Is that right, Mr. Gallant?"

"Yes, but—"

"But what sir?"

"I was wondering if you could tell me-is Mary working tonight?"

"Mary?" The impatient one took a long, disparaging sigh. "Hold on, I'll have to check her schedule." He dropped the phone not too delicately and Jimmy jerked the receiver away from his ear. Oh, great. Someone else is outside the booth waiting.

Jimmy couldn't breathe. He could hear his heart beat. He motioned that he wouldn't be too much longer to the guy waiting, but all he got back was a glare. He jumped as the impatient voice came back on the line.

"Still there, sir?"

"Yes, I am."

The impatient, curt voice sounded so bored and put-upon. "Very well, Mary is scheduled to work tonight."

"Thank you," James squeaked out, sounding like his voice was going into puberty again. Click. The impatient, curt voice hung up.

Later that evening, Jimmy swaggered along the boardwalk on his way to the Chesapeake Crab House. It was a brand new day, a whole new world and he was intent on seeing Mary again. Strutting down the way, he was feeling quite dapper in his new blue shirt, tie, black-and gray checkered vest and navy blue pleated gabardine slacks. he was confident to make a better impression on the waitress named Mary tonight. Mary. Beautiful, shapely, legs-up-to-here Mary. Sarcastic, contemptuous, rude, overbearing Mary. She couldn't stand him. He couldn't get her out of his mind. He could still see her standing over him, her silky, wavy red hair falling across her bare shoulders. Her face was a bronze glow with her turned-up nose and hazel eyes that seemed to peer into his soul. Lips that were created for a lover's kisses. Delicate, fine hands with long manicured fingers that gestured as she spoke, bringing animation and intensity to her words.

As the hostess tried to usher him to a table, he gestured toward the corner he'd occupied last night. A new table sat in place of the three-legged one. "I'm sorry-that table's reserved tonight." He reluctantly took a seat at the table she offered him in the middle of the deck. He thanked her for the menu and eyed the crowded terrace for Mary. The wait staff, as they were the night before, were scrambling here and there but there was no sign of the redhead.

"Well hi there, handsome. Dining all alone tonight?" The curvaceous brunette in the sailor top and culottes loomed over him with order pad in hand, cracking her gum. "I'm Sandy, I'll be your waitress tonight. Can I start you off with a drink?"

"Uh, sure. I'll have a draft please."

"Be right back with that, honey." Sandy Cooke flashed her deep chestnut eyes and spun around to make her way to the bar. Her hips swayed and teased as she walked. His eyes fastened themselves on her for a moment, but soon remembered the reason for his being here tonight. Suddenly, he saw her. It was Mary. On the far corner toward the steps, she was delivering a tray of meals; gorgeous in a soft pink capri outfit with her wavy crimson mane pulled back in a ponytail. James leaned further and further and nearly fell out of his chair.

She joined the other waitress at the bar. Sandy, the brunette, whispered something in Mary's ear that made her laugh and slap Sandy's arm. He snapped his gaze away when the waitress turned and headed back to him.

"There you go, handsome. Now what can I get you to eat? Our specials tonight are mahi mahi quenelles and shrimp scampi, we also have marinated tuna, and our catch of the day is ocean perch with pine nuts. What'll it be?"

"I'll have the eight ounce sirloin. Medium well done, please. With a baked potato and corn."

She squeezed his hand lightly as she retrieved the menu from him. "Not from around here, are ya honey?" Are you one of our brave fightin' boys or just passin' through?"

"U.S. Navy, m'am. Gonna be shipping out on the Forrestal in a few days. Goin' over to 'Nam."

"Gawd, what's this country comin' to?" Her eyebrows rose and her eyes grew larger. "You mean to say they'd send a sweet young thing like you over there in harm's way? That's just a cryin' shame. I mean, it's so dangerous, who knows what those crazies'll do?" Her lips tightened. "Tell you what I think sugar, President Johnson needs to get our guys out of there pronto. Let those Vietnamese settle things for themselves. That's what I'd do." She sighed, holding the menu to her chest. "Well, let me get your order to the cook. I'll be back to check on you in a few, sailor boy." She batted her eyelashes and sauntered off. He picked up the draft and studied it, thinking about Mary, before taking a sip from the glass.

Back in the kitchen, Sandy lit a cigarette and pulled Mary aside. "I'm tellin' you, Missy. That cute little blonde sailor boy is all over me with his eyes. I saw him 'bout starin' a hole in me when we were at the bar a few minutes ago. He's wild about me."

Mary chuckled. "Right, Sandy, whatever you say. Why does it seem that every man who walks into this dump falls head over heels for you? And a sailor to boot?"

"Just you never mind, honey-I guaran-damn-tee it! This one'll be parkin' his shoes under my little ol' bed tonight! She smoothed her short auburn hair and adjusted her top across her narrow waistline. Pulling a compact from her purse that hung on the wall, she powdered her nose, freshened her hot pink lipstick and checked her teeth. "Mmm-hmm…that boy's in for a good time tonight."

The two girls erupted in laughter and hardly noticed the cook trying to reach a pot on a shelf behind them. "Come on, ladies-I'm tryin' ta make a livin' here."

"Oh don't get your shorts in a bunch, Chet. We're just havin' a little fun," Sandy said.

Mary agreed. "You gotta do somethin' to stay sane around this place. She looked at Sandy again and the two convulsed again in fits of giggles.

"Here's your order for table twelve Mary." Chet Randall not amused. Still shaking with laughter, Mary wiped a tear from her eye and transferred the trout almondine and shrimp scampi to her serving tray. "Oh Gawd, Chet, lighten up." Someone patted her fanny as she crossed the tightly-arranged tables to number twelve. She glared at every man that she passed on her way back to the kitchen. "Crap," she said as she remembered that the gluts at table twelve wanted fresh drinks.

"I need two more strawberry daiquiris, Tony." He nodded in response.

Sandy sached up, tapped Mary and pointed a long, slender, manicured finger toward the center of the crowded bistro. "See there, honey. The blonde kid in the blue shirt and checkered vest."

Mary scanned the tables, trying to see beyond the convergence of bluish-gray cigarette smoke rising and the scrambling wait staff. "Nope, I don't see nothin' dolly."

"Oh, come on, look." Annoyed, Sandy took Mary's face in her palms and zeroed her in on James' table. "Right there. Can't you see him? He's right there girl."

In a flash, Mary saw him and recognized him. She felt as though she'd been punched in the stomach hard. She screwed up her face and squinted. "Lord, girly, you sure know how to pick 'em. That loser was here last night. I told you about the sailor moron that practically burned a hole in the deck? That's him."

"Nuh-uh."

"Oh yeah, it is. You better have your fire insurance paid up if you're takin' that one home, kid."

Sandy was not convinced. "So my little sailor boy's isn't the sharpest crayon in the box, he sure is cute isn't he? Sure beats fakin' it another night with fat Tony here."

"Hey," Tony protested, "You know you can't get enough of me."

"Not likely, dog breath. Anyways, tell me you don't think he's cute Mare."

"I think he's a clumsy ninny."

"Well, he's a cute ninny, and that ninny is gettin' lucky tonight."

"Don't say I didn't warn ya, honey." Mary turned away, picked up the drinks and hurried back to table twelve. The people at number six were motioning for her, which posed a problem. The shortest path to them was across the center of the deck, past the "ninny" at table five. She served the daiquiris and was annoyed to see the ninny staring at her, smiling and waving her over. She stiffly marched across the deck toward table six.

"Uh, Miss. Uh, I..." She didn't even glance his way as she strode past. The people at table ten were ready for dessert and coffee. Mary was both irritated and confused by her reaction to the nitwit sailor. Who cared if he did look at her like that? Who cared if Sandy did take him home? Who was he but a ninny that almost scared off all the customers the night before? Confusion always ruffled her feathers a little. Her face flashed almost as crimson as her hair as she scowled at the ninny sailor and took table seventeen's order.

"'Scuse me, I just—" He tried, as she flew past him again. She didn't have the time of day for him. He was everything she knew to avoid; a sailor, handsome, and no doubt, soon to "ship out." She soared past him again as she returned with table seventeen's wedges of key lime pie and black coffee, but Jimmy made no attempt to intercept her this time.

"Here you go, sweetie," the brunette pressed herself against him as she delivered his steak.

"Thanks. That other waitress-the redhead over there-," he motioned toward Mary. "Do you know her very well?"

"Who, Mary?" Her eyes sparked with anger and they shot like arrows across the deck at Mary as Sandy bitterly realized why he asked. "Oh sure, I've known Mary for a long time now. She trained me when I started here about two years ago. Why?" She reached down to straighten his tie and smoothed his wind-blown hair, trying to distract him. "Honey, you really should eat before your food gets cold," she said.

"She's not very friendly."

"Honey, the problem with Mary is, she just doesn't like men." With a feigned puzzled look on her face, she shook her head and brushed closer to him as she placed his plate down before him. Sandy fought hard to contain her fiery temper, but she could barely hold onto her order pad as her hands shook.

He examined her face trying to decide if she was serious, if she was telling the truth. "Are you sure about that? I mean, she's so pretty…"

"Sure as sure can be. It's been known around here for quite some time. You'd better eat that steak while it's still hot-I'll stop by later to see if you need anything." She touched his shoulder. "Can I get you another beer?" She glared toward the kitchen where Mary had gone, then smiled back at him.

"Yeah, I guess so…" Right now, James couldn't be more confused or disappointed. If what she was telling him were true, he didn't stand a chance of getting to know the redhead. But something was telling him that all was not as it seemed. But why would this gal lie to him about a thing like that?

At the bar, Sandy complained to Tony. "That little slut Mary. She double-crossed me. I can't believe it. She knew I liked that sailor and she's been puttin' the moves on him behind my back. All this time she's goin', "he's a nitwit. He's a loser. You don't want him." but really she's set her sights on him. What kinda friend does that? Gimme another draft, Tony." He rolled his eyes and grabbed a glass. She continued on, "I can't believe she'd pull this on me again. After all the time we've been friends… you know what I say? With friends like her, who needs enemies? Hurry up with that, Tony." She was possessively eyeing Jim at his table, but Mary hadn't emerged from the kitchen yet. The bartender sat the glass of amber, foamy beer on her tray.

"What are you goin' on about? You two aren't friends," Tony said. You don't give her the time of day outside 'a this dump. You never even see her except here. Don't you think she knows how many times you've asked everyone from work except her over for one of your beer parties? You know as well as I do that you don't like her because you know she's prettier than you."

"Shove it, you damned liar!" She hurled the full glass against the back wall of the bar as Tony ducked to get out of the way. The clamor of the busy diner covered the noise. "Give me another one, and shut up, you moron. You don't know anything. Gawd, I hate you both." Her chest heaved with fury and the tray was shaking in her hands. Mary was not going to screw this up for her. Not this time.

****

Sandy's fury gripped her. Suddenly she was twelve years old again. She watched from the kitchen window as they all got into the station wagon. They even waved as the car backed out of the driveway. They couldn't see the tears she wiped from her cheeks or feel the emptiness inside her, not that they'd have cared if they did.

It was August 20th and her mother and two older sisters were on their way to shop for school clothes. Only ten minutes ago Sandy tried her best to convince her mother.

"Mama, couldn't I go this year?" It was a question that she'd asked last year too. She asked it every year. And the answer was always "No. Sandy, you have plenty of clothes to wear this year. I bet there's lots of kids in your class that would die to have all the clothes you're going to be wearing."

"But they aren't mine. They're Cindy and Joanne's clothes. The girls at school always know about them and tease me."

Her mother knelt down. "Just what do you expect me to buy them with?" She tightly cupped Sandy's tear-covered cheeks in her hands. "God, Sandy. Don't you think I feel guilty enough to make you wear their hand-me-downs? Why do you have to put me through this every year?"

Sandy's tears became sobs. Her mother continued, "They're perfectly good clothes and you're only a year behind the twins. As much as I love you Sandy, the girls are so pretty. The school and our church really make over them. It's high time you understand that you just weren't the lucky one, honey. Not all girls can be popular. But you'll find your place someday. I just know it. If you don't get the looks maybe you'll end up with the "brains." With that, she patted Sandy on the head and walked away.

****

"Here you go, honey. Everything okay? Why, I just realized that you know my name but I never got yours."

"Jimmy Gallant." He answered her but his mind was on Mary.

"Well, Jimmy Gallant, is your steak all right?" She toyed with the silver plated chain around her neck. What did she have to do to get through to him? He acted as if she didn't exist. He just kept looking past her for that damned Mary.

"Yes, it's fine." A customer at table three was motioning for her. She nodded at them, annoyed, and softly scratched the back of his neck. "Now if you need anything else I'll be around, okay?"

He nodded as she huffed and stormed off. Jimmy continued to eat, spying out the crowd for a glimpse of her. From time to time, he'd spot her and their eyes would fix on one another. But her's were looks of contempt. As much as she tried to ignore him, it unnerved her that he was staring at her. She kept making stupid mistakes on orders, something she never did, and tips were going down from fives and tens to a few dollars.

"Miss, I didn't order that." The annoyed tourist protested. Mary checked her pad again. "Oh, I'm sorry..." She grabbed the plate and scurried over to table seven.

"I didn't want fries-I told you, baked potato." She flipped a page on her pad.

"Lady, I've got it right here-mahi mahi with—oh, baked potato." She was losing her grip, also something she never did. "Look, this place is crazy tonight. Cut me a break and eat the stupid fries, please?" The elderly woman stared at her husband across the table, then glared back at Mary.

"I wanted a baked potato, young lady. Please take this away and bring back the right thing."

"Yeah, bring back the right thing." The husband waved Mary off.

"Fine. I'll be back..." she raced for the kitchen with the plate. This had to stop.

That crummy sailor was ruining her whole night. Might as well have stayed home. Back in the kitchen, she leaned against the counter and took a deep breath.

The doors swung open and the fully-loaded busboy's cart careened through and smashed into the back of her ankles hard.

"Yow!" She screamed. "What the..." Sweat broke out on her forehead and the room started to go black as tears welled up in her eyes. Then she turned and saw Sandy, seething in the doorway.

"What'd ya do that for? You crazy or somethin'?"

"You slut. You dirty, sneaky little slut!"

Mary pushed the cart full of dishes away from her, breathing deeply and trying to not pass out. "What's wrong with you?"

"You know exactly what's wrong with me."

Mary gasped for air. "What's wrong with you is that you're about to get your lights knocked out, you crazy little—"

"You knew. You knew I was int'rested in that cute sailor."

"What are you talkin' about?" Mary was still dazed.

"You knew I liked that guy at table five and you've been puttin' the moves on him behind my back. All this time you're goin', "Oh-he's a nitwit. He's a loser. You don't want him..." Sandy took advantage of the fact that the taller, stronger woman was still in a state of shock. She shoved Mary against the cupboard.

"Stop it! You're a nut case!" Mary warned.

"Yeah? Here's a nut case for ya." She lunged and grabbed hold of Mary's ponytail and slapped her across the face.

"You crazy..." Mary pushed her back, and Sandy tumbled over the plastic waste cans full of souring table scraps and litter. She leapt to her feet and grabbed the closest thing to her, a cast iron skillet on the counter. Mary turned for a moment to see if anyone was within earshot to help her calm Sandy down.

"Aghhh!" She charged Mary with it and swung, hitting her upside the head with it. Stunned, Mary stumbled backwards and leaned against an empty cart, reaching up to feel the goose egg growing on her forehead and feeling the flow of blood. Sandy dropped the skillet and began scratching and ripping at Mary's face and clothing.

"Stop!" Mary tried to push Sandy away, but she was being pummeled by Sandy's angry fists and gouged by Sandy's long, sharp red nails.

"I hate you! You bitch!" Sandy raged.

A flurry of slaps and pushes ensued, but after a few seconds, Mary'd had enough. She drew back her fist, grabbed Sandy by the scruff of her neck, and decked her. Her fist connected hard with the girl's jaw, propelling her back into the corner where the trash cans of fermenting trash lay. With that, Chet finally heard the commotion and raced across the kitchen from his grill as Tommy McGee, one of the waiters came running into the kitchen.

"What the... Mary, what'd ya do that for?" She was leaning against the counter, trying to catch her breath and wiping blood from her head with a towel.

"She's crazy, Chet. I don't know if she got hold of some bad weed and smoked it, or what. She attacked me for no reason."

The men lifted the sleeping Sandy from the spilled garbage. She reeked. Wiping the greasy, fishy table scraps from her face, and pulling fragments of shellfish and gobs of shrimp cocktail from her matted hair, they patted her cheeks.

"Wake up Sandy. Come on." She was out of it. Chet glared at Mary. "I hope you didn't kill her. How many times have you had a hen fight with one of the girls, Mary. You say she started it? You say she attacked you?." He made no attempt to hide his doubt.

"Yeah."

"We'll have to wait 'til she comes around and get her side of the story too. You'd better clean up and go home for the night. I can't have this goin' on around here and you know it." Curious waitresses and waiters were crowding the door for a view. "When you s'posed to work again, kid?" He asked.

"Tomorrow."

"Okay, come back then and we'll talk about it."

"All right, all right, whatever you say. But she's crazy." Mary tasted blood and felt the goose egg on her forehead again. "I'll see ya tomorrow, Chet."

"Oh, and Mary?"

"Yeah?"

"Go out the other way, I don't want the customers seein' you like that."

Jimmy was surprised when a waiter brought him his check instead of the brunette. "What happened to the girl?"

The waiter slapped the check down on the table and rushed off, his hands in the air. "Don't ask, mister. Just don't ask."

****

It took every last ounce of effort for her to pick her head up from the sofa pillow and ask me, "What're you doin' home so early?"

"I'm not that early, Mother." I picked up the empty bottle of scotch. "Was this full when you started?"

"Maybe it was, and maybe it wasn't," she slurred. "What's it to you? 'Sides, I asked you a question." She tried to focus at a clock on the wall.

"I just got off early, that's all." I threw my handbag on the coffee table and sunk down in the old musty, lumpy armchair.

"You never get off early at that dump. You're up to somethin', aren't you? What'd ya do, start trouble with one of the girls again?" Even though I was used to it, I hated to come home and find her in this condition, with her wanting to interrogate me.

"Well, it was slow tonight, so I left early, okay?"

"Don't get huffy with me, girlie. You show your mother a little respect. Mary honey, get me a glass of water and a couple aspirins, will ya? My head is throbbin'."

"Mother, I just sat down. I'm tired." She just grinned and gave me one of those be-a-good-little-girl looks that I despise. Ugh! I hate this. Seems like we've played this scene over and over all my life.

THEY NEVER REALLY LEAVE

"Come on, honey. Frankie said he might come by this evening. I don't want to be bad company because of a headache." Like being sloshed would be such good company.

I didn't move. I just sat there, glaring in disgust. She lay slumped across on the sofa in her crumpled, dingy slip, a cigarette with a long ash sticking out of the corner of her mouth.

"You better watch that ash, it's gonna fall on the carpet."

"Who cares about this ratty old carpet." she tried to focus on the ashtray and gave her cigarette a flick. "Mary, honey please, Mama's got a sick headache. Go get me some aspirins."

"Oh crap Mother." I pulled my tired, bruised aching body out of the chair and went into the kitchen to get the pills.

"Oh, jeeze…" The kitchen was a disaster zone. She must have been attempting to prepare her precious Frank something to eat. The sink was full of blackened pots and greasy fry pans. Blood from a ground beef container was oozing down and pooling at the end of the counter. There were cans of half-opened tomato sauce and the thick syrup from an overturned can of kidney beans encircled the toaster where it appeared she'd tried to cram thick cut pieces of bread in it. "Mom, what were you tryin' to do out here?"

"Mom?"

"What, Mary?"

"What's up with the mess in the kitchen?"

"Oh that. I think the can opener's broken again. Can you take a look at it, or maybe I can have Frankie fix it for me."

"Yeah, like he fixed the toilet last week?"

"I don't know Mary. Just bring me the damned aspirins girl."

"I'm sure you expect me to clean this mess up before he comes." I already knew the answer, the same as always.

I filled a glass from the kitchen tap, shook my head at the mess that lay before me, walked into the living room and slapped two aspirins in her hand. "Oh honey, you're such a good girl—hey, you're a mess. Just look at you." She struggled to focus on me. You did get into another scrap with one of those girls, didn't you?"

"You'd better get dressed if you're getting company."

"What company-it's only Frankie. He's seen me in less than this."

"Oh please, mother." She relished embarrassing me, especially in front of Frank or anyone else when she was drinkin'.

"Well he has." And you just better be nicer to him-he might be your step-daddy someday. I think he's gonna marry me soon." She laid her head back against the arm of the sofa and rubbed her temples.

"I wouldn't hold my breath, if I was you."

"If you were me? If you were me?" She shot up from the sunken couch in an instant sober rage. "I'll tell you somethin', missy, if you were me you'd deserve to have a little pleasure in your life after all I've been through in my life. You wouldn't last a minute being me. How dare you talk to me like that? You'd have grown up in an orphanage if it weren't for me. They told me to get rid of you. They told me to let those people have you. They said I'd never make ends meet. They said I'd be sorry if I kept you." Her rage turned to tears and she collapsed onto the sofa again. I just stared at her-I'd heard this pitiful argument time after time since I was little. Pretty near every time she'd get drunk. "You're all I got, Mary. You're all I ever had. And all you ever had was me. Don't you see it? It's just me and you, and that's the way it'll probably always be. Come over here and let mama hold you for a minute." I begrudgingly sat down on the couch beside her. She grabbed my head and pulled it to her neck, rocking me gently, soaking my top with her tears. She reeked of whiskey. "Just you 'n me. You 'n me. Mary and her mama… all alone. Just you 'n me." She turned her head to sob into my neck and rocked herself back to sleep.

Chapter 2

I edged my Monte Carlo to the curb as she pulled in the drive at the second house from the end. The little row houses looked nearly identical along Fulton Street-all weatherworn and in various stages of decay, with scraggly palm trees and tufts of sun-burnt sea grass in well-kept but sandy, arid yards. I hoped she didn't spot me following her from the restaurant. It wasn't easy keeping up with her, with her speeding along at 50 in the 35 mph zones, and the way she sped through amber lights.

What was I doing anyway? I'd never followed anybody before. I leaned forward in my seat and watched the upstairs windows of the faded gray house she'd entered. A light came on in the side room, then was turned back off. It seems like hours passed as I waited, and a brighter light came on in the window facing the street. My resolve is beginning to weaken. What if she knew I'd followed her? Maybe she called the cops already. It hasn't been long enough since Chief Galley had to come down to the Virginia Beach Police Department to bail me and four buddies out after we'd been arrested for bustin' up the Riptide Bar. He'd really have my tail in a sling if he found me in trouble again. But those hippies at the Riptide had it coming to them. Bunch of flippin' beatniks, talking down America and the whole military, saying we were all ignorant war mongers and saying that we had no business going over to Vietnam. Losers. We had just been shootin' the breeze in our quarters on the ship about the reports of the anti-war demonstrations on the radio before we went out on the town. A few too many drinks, and then after listening to those long-haired weirdos, and our fists had a field day. We offered to pay for the damages, anyway. It was hard to listen to people talk down about our country when we were about to sail off and risk our lives protecting her. America-love it or leave it, that's what I say.

I didn't know what was going on up there but I couldn't sit any longer. I got out and began to amble toward her house. A shaggy mutt in the window of a house barks and I just about jumped out of my skin. The porch light comes on and an old unshaven black guy peeked his head around the curtain and watches me for a minute, then shoos the dog out of the window. My heart was in my throat as I edged closer to her house. I stopped as she appeared in the front window, then turned away. I heard arguing, women arguing. One voice was Mary's.

Could the other waitress be right, you know, about her not liking men? Mary acted like she hated not only men but most everybody. She was a knockout. I paused and look back down the street, now a couple blocks from the safety of my car. Okay, be cool, I said to myself. Your head's just playin' games with you. You don't know who the other voice is up there. Oh crap! I tripped and almost fell on the uneven sidewalk. I felt a raindrop on my arm, then another and another. The sky broke open and dumped on me, soaking me to the bone. I should go back. The road's drainage can't keep up with the deluge, and four inches of water fills the street. I was completely soaked as the sidewalk also floods over. I saw her again in the front window. Looks like a kitchen, with potted plants lining the sill. She looked grim. Seems like she's washing dishes or something. Isn't that peachy, she comes home from a hard day's work and has to clean up the kitchen while who knows who lays on the couch. The rain passed but the street and sidewalks were still flooded. A tidal wave roared over me as an idiot in a '59 Chevy cut through the water in the street. Great. Just great. I wiped my face on my soaked sleeve. It was hard to see through the steamed-up window. Yeah, it's her. I could barely make out her scarlet locks as they're reflected in the soft light. Why am I so drawn to this rude redheaded waitress? She doesn't even like me. In fact, I think she hates me. You know what? I don't even know why she hates me. Tonight at the diner she wouldn't even stop by my table or acknowledge me. She was ignoring me on purpose. Hard to get, maybe? No, there's more… I just know there's more to my beautiful Mary than what I've seen. I grin because I was already calling her "my Mary." How could someone so beautiful have such a storm raging within her? She can't be so bitter for no reason. Someone's hurt her, like real bad. Some loser, and he probably got her hopes all up and then dumped her for another girl. That would make any woman hate men. There are a thousand possibilities for what could have happened. How I'd love to break through her tough exterior and see what's really inside. If she'd only give me a chance. It seems hopeless; I feel hopeless, as I crouched like a drowned rat beneath the window of a woman who I think I might love. Suddenly, a delicate, soapy hand comes to the window to wipe it clear and she sees me.

****

What next? I come home from a long day's work, find my kitchen in a hovel and Mother draped across the sofa, drunk as a skunk, and now that dopey sailor is standing outside my window, soaking wet. I can't freakin' believe it. How did he find out where I live? If Chet or Tony told him, I'll kill 'em. I wiped my hands on the dish towel. Just what does he want from me? What am I supposed to do-feel sorry for the little wet pup? Oh, sure. I'll bring him up and introduce him to my half-dressed, soused mother and say, "Hey Mom, I want you to meet this guy who got me into a fight and almost fired tonight at work. And, by the way, Mom, he's a sailor." That'll send her into a grand new tirade. I want to look again, to see if maybe he got smart and took off. But I don't want to look, he'll think I'm interested in him if I do. But I have to know if he's still down there. Fat ole Frankie'll be pulling up in his clunker any minute, and with his nosiness, Mother will have the whole story in five minutes flat. He'll probably drag the boy up here- "Hey Margie, meet your daughter's latest flame. Oh, he's a fine boy, one of our nation's defenders of freedom. Yessiree, United States Navy. Are you gettin' this honey, Mary has herself a new sailor boyfriend."

She'll hit the roof. I don't even have the kitchen cleaned up yet. Ugh, what is in that green bowl? Whatever it is, it sure smells bad. It'd serve Frankie right to have to eat mother's cooking for a change.

Should I look? Oh, God, I hate this. Why do things like this have to happen to me? Okay, what if I make it look like I just happen to accidentally look down there again, kind of nonchalantly. I lean over the sink and peer down...

"Mary, what're ya lookin' at?" Holy smokes, she scared me.

"God, Mother, why do you sneak up on me like that?"

"I wasn't sneakin' up on no one. What're ya lookin' at?" She tries to shoo me away from the window but I hold my ground.

"Oh, nothin'. There's a dog down there that got caught in the rain. Think I'll grab some towels and go down and help the little fella out." Her face screws up in confusion.

"A dog, you say?"

"Yes, mother, just a dog." I turn her around and point her toward her room. "Why don't you please get dressed now. You don't want Frankie seeing you like this." I push her out of the kitchen and rush to the bathroom for some towels. "I'll be right back up."

"I didn't think you even liked dogs..." She says as she staggers toward her room.

I'm frantic. I race down the steps, drag him into the carport and throw the pile of towels at him. "Just what'n sam hell do you think you're doin' here?"

"I don't know-I mean, I didn't get a chance to talk to you tonight at the restaurant." I look nervously upstairs, expecting mother to come out of the door any moment.

"Now just why would we need to talk?" He's shaking from the cold rain, trying to dry off with the towels. His wet tee shirt and slacks stick to his firm, athletic body. I still don't like him.

"I thought maybe I could apologize for the inconvenience I caused you last night." He did a double-take . Uh, did you know that you have a black eye?" My hand shot to cover my face, I'd forgotten about my war wounds.

"Look, kid, why don't you do us both a favor and take a powder?" I watch him towel dry his blond hair. "This ain't goin' nowhere-for one thing, I'm old enough to be, well, your older sister." I never noticed how blue his eyes were before. "Besides that, what kind of a bimbo do you take me for? You sailors are all the same. Pull into port and think you gotta pick up the first girl you see." He sure is young. "Now, you may be a nice guy and all that, but I'm just not interested. Understand?" A boy, but he's built like a man-his biceps flex as he dries the back of his head. I pull my eyes away, taking a deep breath and exhaling slowly.

"Mary. Mary… I need your help…" My soused mother calls from upstairs.

"Just a minute, Mom, almost done down here…" He looks at me, puzzled. He takes off his shoes and wrings his socks out. "Look, buddy, give me a break, okay?" He's not moving fast enough and I grab a towel. Have to hurry him up. Should I—I don't know where to dry him. I start at his neck and pat down to his chest. Oh God, he's watching me. Those eyes. Those steel blue eyes. He holds my hand to his chest.

"You know, I couldn't take my eyes off you from the instant I first saw you."

"Don't say that."

"It's true." He still grips my hand to his chest. I try to pull it away, but he's strong.

"Why can't you give me a chance?" I struggle with him to break free from his grip. Mother, please don't come out here now!

"Let go. You're just a kid, darn it. And you're a sailor. What do you think, I'm hard up, or something?"

"No, but what's all this about being a sailor, anyways?" I'm still prying his hands off mine.

"You're all the same, that's what. No account, here today-gone tomorrow, one night stand lover boys who think they're God's gift." Wounded, he lets me go.

"Is that what you think about me?"

"Yeah, well, I don't know." I panic again as I think about mother upstairs. "I gotta go-you'd better take off now." I push him out of the carport toward the flooded street.

"Who told you sailors were no good?" He grabs me by the arms again.

"Let go of me!" I break free from him. (Jeeze, this kid just doesn't quit!)

"I want you to tell me why you think I'm a bum just because I'm a sailor."

"Look, I'm not going to stand out here in this weather and debate this with you. Just get a move on, will ya? I have to go help my mother," I reply.

"Oh, that's your mother you were arguing with up there."

"Yeah, so? Look kid, I already got enough problems, okay?"

"Tell me why you won't go out with me—"

I'm really getting fired up now. "I just don't go out with sailors, okay?" I answered. "Now get yourself out of here!"

"Why?" He demanded. "Why don't you date sailors?" He wouldn't quit! He just wouldn't quit.

"None of your business, that's why! Where's your car?" I say as I'm frantically looking up and down the street.

"Mary, if you'd just give me a chance, you might just like me. I think you could even love me, if you tried." I turn to walk away. "Come on, Mary, one date. If you don't enjoy yourself, I swear, I'll bug off and leave you alone. I can't stop thinkin' about you."

"I have to go. And you have to go," I ordered him. I start up the steps.

"You're so—"

"I'm leaving now, go home, or back to your ship, or wherever you people go," I demanded. I drop a towel as I keep climbing the stairs. He catches it as it falls to the ground and gently hands it to me.

"You're beautiful." I stop in my tracks, turn and point an angry finger at him. I suddenly realize that it's been forever since anyone said that to me.

"You-you go on now. Get out of here. There's nothing here for you," my voice shaking now.

"Mary, you're beautiful."

Again? He said it again? My hands are trembling. He sees the tears welling up in my eyes. I hate it when I get mad enough that I cry.

"Just give me your phone number and you can go back to whatever you were doing; you're beautiful, and I'd like to get to know you."

I cross my arms and shiver with a combination of laughter and tears, "Just like the song says, huh?" He smiles out of the corner of his mouth and seduces me with those piercing blue eyes.

"Yeah, baby. Just like the song says."

"Look, Jimmy, this just isn't happening. You go find someone else. I've been down this dead-end road enough times." I reach the first landing on the steps, glaring at him as I go. No way I'm getting hurt again.

"So how about it, what's your number?" I'm thinking this is crazy. I'm thinking he's really cute, and that he's really beginning to fascinate me. But no way I'm giving him my number.

"Come on, gorgeous. Give me another chance, please."

"585-4242." As I bolt for the steps, he claps his hands once and shouts.

"I'll call you tomorrow, okay?" I keep running up the steps and don't answer.

****

The courtship of James Lee Gallant and Mary Bauer began on a balmy Friday evening in July at Martine'es in Virginia Beach. Hesitant to introduce Jim to her mother, Mary insisted they meet at the chic French restaurant. He was waiting in his black '63 Monte Carlo, listening with anticipation to the Turtle's hit song "Happy Together" when she pulled in the lot in her red Mustang at 7:50.

Jim leapt from his car and raced to open her door as soon as he spotted her. "Dang!" he gasped. "You look stunning!" She emerged dressed in a black velvet miniskirt and rather low-cut black satin blouse with spaghetti straps that more than flattered her exquisite figure.

"Sorry I'm late, it's my mother, she—" The whole truth was that Mary's stomach had been tied up in knots all day. She almost stayed at home.

"It's alright, believe me, I know how parents can be."

"Well, it's a long story and I'm sure—"

"Look, it's okay, Mary." Offering his arm, he added, "this is our night; we're not going to let your mom or anyone else make us uptight and ruin it, okay?" He smiled that cute right-sided smirk again and put her at ease.

Hmmm... You look quite handsome yourself tonight, Mr. Gallant, she said to herself. He did look dashing in his indigo suit, freshly laundered and starched white shirt, and blue/gray tie. The seventy-five degree humid evening air carried with it the aroma of foods cooking in the kitchen of the restaurant as they crossed the lot to the front door.

As they sat opposite one another at a cozy, secluded corner table, the candlelight flickered away at their attractive young faces. It seemed like it were their very first meeting. As though their disastrous first meeting had never happened. They were reborn in the ambience of the evening. She marveled to herself how he made her feel so comfortable, so at ease. He smiled at her dry sense of humor, and yet delicate, feminine grace. Was this really the same girl as the one who'd made a fool of him a few days earlier? She had been harsh as the December wind in Jamestown; now she was soft, radiant, and incredibly beautiful.

After they ordered and the white wine was poured, Jimmy proposed a toast: "To new beginnings," his deep blue eyes dancing in the flickering candlelight.

She concurred, "To new beginnings." They sipped their wine. Silence fell upon them as though an unspoken pact had been agreed upon not to alloy the moment with forced small talk or empty conversation. Several minutes passed as they exchanged glances and smiles that required no words. It wasn't a nervous, uncomfortable quiet as one might encounter on a blind date gone bad, but more of an un-uttered language that was theirs alone, one in which they were each inherently fluent. She was, much to her own malcontent, becoming as enamored with him as he already was with her.

When their meals arrived, so did their conversation. Almost in torrents, at first, as though each had this voracious need to know everything about each other all at once; about their life, family, hopes and dreams. They were soon in laughter between bites of food as they exchanged funny anecdotes about their past. To learn that each was an "only child" was uncanny, but when they realized that they shared the experience of living with an alcoholic parent, the bond between them grew even stronger. They well understood how difficult it was at times in each other's homes. They both confessed of their longing to escape despite feelings of being held captive to feelings of guilt and the responsibility to stay. It seemed so easy to talk to him, Mary marveled. Wait a minute. This is going way too well, she thought. She said nothing more as they finished their dinner.

The band started playing a tender love song and he asked, "Would you like to dance?" As they took to the dance floor, their bodies seemed to meld together as he held her close and she rested her head on his shoulder. "Baby, I need your lovin'-Got to have all your lovin,'" he was singing quietly along with the band. He held her so tenderly, like one would a delicate, precious treasure. He breathed in the soft sweet fragrance of her long, wavy scarlet hair as it draped her bare shoulders. She was delicious in every sense of the word, and he was finally holding her in his arms. They continued to sway through the next song and the next and the next. When he drew back to ask her if she'd like to sit awhile, her eyes were pools of tears.

"What's wrong, Mary?" Embarrassed at being found out, she dashed for her seat and wiped her eyes with a handkerchief from her purse.

"Mary, what's goin' on?" He was wounded by her tears, as though he was responsible for them.

She reassured him, shaking her head sadly. "It's not you, Jimmy. It's not you." He pulled his chair over close to hers.

"If it's not something I did or said, then what was it? Whatever it is, angel, I'll fix it, or I'll make it up to you somehow. I just want to help you. I just want to be with you."

"It's nothing that can be fixed. It doesn't concern you-it's my problem." She stared down in shame at the table, avoiding his eyes. The demons from her past had just arrived in time to ruin what had been a perfect evening. They never left her alone for long.

"Ah, come here, angel." He leaned closer to embrace her. She sobbed on his shoulder until it soaked clear through to his skin. "It's okay, it's gonna be okay. I'm going to take care of you. I love you, Mary."

"What?" She pushed him away violently. "Don't say that-don't you tell me that! Don't you dare try to pull that one on me! Why'd you have to—" Her eyes brimmed with distrust. "I'll be back."

"Where're you going?" he asked, confused.

"Just to the ladies' room." And with that she crossed the room, leaving behind a very perplexed young man. He watched her walk away, then seemed to be held in a trance watching the spot where she'd vanished from sight. He just sat there, transfixed, bewildered, like a small child lost in a busy shopping mall, unable to find his mother. Was she coming back? Was she all right? Should he go after her?

"Is everything alright, sir?" The waiter broke his concentration, but he answered without looking up.

"Yes, everything's okay."

"Would you and the lady care for dessert, sir?"

"Huh? Oh, I don't know. I'll ask her when she comes back. The waiter gave him a cursory smile and sauntered off.

Jimmy waited and waited for what seemed like hours for her return. He looked at his watch, she'd been gone at least half an hour, maybe forty-five minutes. He finally imposed on a waitress to check the ladies' room and make sure Mary was all right.

"Nobody's in there, sir."

"No, you must be mistaken. Are you sure?"

"Yes, sir. No one."

"Is there an exit to the outside in there?"

"Well, yeah, there's an old service door in the back but no one ever uses it."

"Thank you very much. Waiter, my check please." He paid the bill and raced to the parking lot. Sure enough, her car was gone. Under his windshield wiper he found a note that read "I'm sorry. Can't do this."

****

I'm so confused, I can't for the life of me understand what I did wrong. Everything was going great until I told her I loved her. Aren't people generally happy, or at least flattered when they're told that? Not Mary-she was mortified. It's not like I say that to every girl I date- actually she's the only girl I've dated that I've ever said that to. But how am I ever going to get her to believe that?

I drive back to Fulton Street. Sure enough, there sits her red mustang. I pull over behind it and let the car idle for a few minutes. No lights on in her house. Man! I thought she was actually starting to like me. There's a huge globe of a full moon cresting over the Atlantic, casting its shimmering reflection across the waves-would have been the perfect evening for a romantic walk along the beach together. I see a slight rustling of the curtains in her kitchen, then nothing. Nothing else to do but head back to the base.

I wake up the next morning feeling even more tired than when I laid down. Oh, yeah. It's because of the dream:

In the dream, Mary and I are getting married. She's a beautiful sight, coming down the aisle in white lace and veils. Everyone is overjoyed, Mom, Dad, even her mom. We dash to the car as rice rains down on us. What a perfect day-I finally have my Mary. I love her, and she loves me. We honeymoon in the Florida keys where we walk moonlit beaches by night, then make mad love in our suite and sleep in the next day.

We call our parents and get a big surprise. My dad and her mom have both gone into AA and neither has had a drink all week. Mom was so excited to tell me about it that she cried. Her and dad are coming to Florida next month for a second honeymoon. Margie-Mary's mom-is going to enroll in a beauty school and get a regular job. Everything is finally turning around for all of us.

When we return home, I get notice that I'm to be assigned shore duty in Norfolk for the next four years of my enlistment. As much as I love the Forrestal, I'm glad to be off the ship for a while. Mary and I go house-hunting and look at several places. After a few weeks, we have it narrowed down to two houses, one is a modern condominium on the beach, the other a nice four-bedroom tudor in Norfolk. After a few months of living in base housing, she's really eager to find a real home. It's a big step I say, buying a house, so let's make sure we hold out and get what we really like.

One day when I come home, Mary meets me at the door all excited. She saw one on the television, and can we go look at it after dinner? She has the address in hand, so I say of course we can go. We drive out to Portsmouth and locate the three-bedroom Victorian at 10 Cole Avenue-just a few blocks from Portsmouth Naval Hospital. I pull the car over to the curb across from it and we're awestruck with its beauty. It's painted in off white, mauve and deep burgundy. There's a huge porch that stretches all the way around from the front to the side, must be 15 feet wide. Mary loves porches, and she never had one that big. We have to get out of the car and have a closer look.

The front lawn is manicured and landscaped with style, a tall oak standing guard by the street and lush evergreen shrubs and white azaleas in bloom hugging the front of the home. Out back, we find a spacious, rolling green lawn that is home to a giant of a weeping willow, a gazebo painted in the colors of the house, a small pond and several perennial gardens that are situated so that you can meander from one to the next along a soft bark/mulch path. We're loving it and we haven't even seen the inside yet!

When I finally drag her back to the car, Mary is chattering non-stop the whole way home, remember the willow tree-wouldn't it be fine to sit in the gazebo on warm summer evenings, and oh, the porch-isn't it just perfect… We're both disappointed when the realtor has closed for the day when we try to call them, but I leave a message with our number.

The next day, I come home in a bad mood. Unusual for me or for

THEY NEVER REALLY LEAVE

Mary. Nothing seemed to go right at work and they denied the leave that I put in for to move, if we get that house. While I eat my dinner, Mary paces like a mother cat about to give birth; she's too excited to eat. The realtor called back, and will show the house at 6 p.m. I'm grumpy and she gets upset. Do I want to cancel the appointment? We need to decide now because they'll be out of the office and on their way there by 5:30. No, I don't want to cancel the appointment. I tell her the bad news about my leave. She assures me that we'll work it all out somehow, hugs my neck and kisses me on the forehead. My mood takes a turn for the better.

On the way to Portsmouth, we agree that if the interior of the house is in bad shape that it won't be a good choice for us. I can do a few minor repairs, plumbing and maybe a little rewiring, but should the floors, ceilings or walls need costly repairs, we'll have to pass on the house. I'll need to work on them over the price, because I can't go over twenty-four nine, tops. They're asking thirty-five. We'll offer them twenty-two to start, if we want the house.

We want the house. The leaded glass door opens into a stately foyer with a crystal chandelier. The living room, den, and master bedroom each have ornate old open fireplaces. There's not a crack or a sag to be found in any ceiling or wall, and the hardwood floors throughout are polished to a shine and sturdy. The kitchen is modern with light oak cabinets and lots of counter space, and there's even an automatic dishwasher. I tease Mary and say we won't be able to use it because it'll cost to much in electricity to run it. She gets that look like she gets when she's about to itemize seventy reasons in order of importance for why we will have to have an automatic dishwasher, then realizes that I'm pulling her leg and pokes me in the ribs.

So, we love the house and Mary's convinced that the house loves us back. We make an offer of twenty-two and they turn us down. We offer twenty-four and they accept it. We'll close in four months, but if my wife has her way, it'll be two.

Mary again prevails and we move into the new house two months and three days later. We both love it. The first day, I even carry her over the threshhold and we make mad love all night on a blanket on the floor.

We'll worry about moving the furniture tomorrow, she says.

About two months later, Mary thinks she's pregnant and goes to the base clinic, where the doctor there confirms it. Life is good-I'm going to be a daddy! What joy we feel when our daughter arrives, just a few weeks early. We name her Deborah Jean. I have two angels now! Mary is such a good mother and dotes constantly over our daughter, having fun dressing her up and taking her out to show her off. We visit our families on the holidays, and they of course also adore the baby. It's amazing to watch how fast she grows, too. I love coming home to my two girls, and before I know it, Debbie is three and her mother says she's going to have another baby.

This is a more difficult pregnancy for Mary. She's not well most of the time, and has to spend days on end in bed. I call and get a temporary housekeeper/nanny. When finally the strenuous months have passed, young Timothy Lee Gallant makes a triumphant entry into this world at 8 lbs, 7 oz. My son! Debbie was so excited when her mom and new brother came home from the hospital, she thought it was her baby and wouldn't let him out of her sight.

Mary is still acting peculiar. I can't put it into words, but it's almost like she's not as excited over Timmy as she was with Debbie. I try to talk to her about it but she won't tell me what's wrong. I ask her if she wants to keep the housekeeper on a permanent basis and she says no. Every night when I try to touch her she turns away from me to face the wall. She seems to only be doing only the minimum effort for the children, rather than doting over them and preening as she'd done before with Debbie. I worry each day what has happened to my loving, enthusiastic Mary.

One day, I come home to find my worst fears realized. Debbie happily comes running to meet me at the door, covered from head to toe in chocolate-she's harvested a full bag of chocolate chips from the fridge. I call out to Mary but there's no answer. I carry Debbie upstairs, wash her up and change her clothes, then go in to check on Timmy, who is now five months old.

He's safe and sound asleep in his crib, but a note pinned to his diaper reads "I'm sorry. Can't do this."

THEY NEVER REALLY LEAVE

****

I never expected him to understand—how could he know the things that have gone on in my life? I'd hate it if he did know. Why can't I leave it all in the past where it belongs and move on with my life? God, if only I could. Maybe then I'd stop waking up screaming and crying in the night. Maybe then I could learn what it really means to trust a man. Poor guy-I was wrong to lead him on the way I did. It's just that it felt so easy, so comfortable when I was with him. He made me feel like I didn't have a past, and only the present mattered. But I should have known better, I knew the whole thing was impossible, I was just fooling myself. He must hate me now. I sure have a talent for destroying things. If there ever were a man that I could see myself trying to make a life with, it would be him.

Oh, mother! If only you would have known, if only you could have protected me. If you'd have realized what all those men did to me each night when you passed out after they'd finished with you, would you have been strong enough to prevent it? What a dumb kid I was—I used to think that they had your permission to come into my room. What kind of mother would allow that to go on if she were aware of it? It would kill you now if I ever told you.

Have you ever felt like your life wasn't real, like it was only a dream and that someday you'd miraculously wake up and discover that none of it had taken place? I used to pretend that my life wasn't real and that one morning I would awaken in a fancy house with a real mom and a real dad and laugh at myself for having had such a silly dream.

I wish that I would have known my father. To have at least met him once, or to have received one letter or a birthday card. It hurts to realize that he knows I'm out there somewhere and he doesn't even care. Mom has always said that all sailors were that way. I wonder what there was about him that made her trust him. How did she feel when she realized that she was pregnant, and that he was never coming back for her? Did she think I didn't realize from a very young age that I was a "mistake?"

Did she hate me too?

I'm such a dope. There he goes down the street, the one guy I've ever met that really seemed to care. Now I've driven him away from me. If I had half a brain, I'd chase those taillights all the way back to the base. But oh, no-not Mary. Not Mary, the girl who hates men. Mary the loner who turns down every invitation to every party, more content to stay at home and babysit my drunken mother rather than take another chance that I could have a life. I've been burned too many times—first by my father the sailor, then by so many others, including several sailors that my mom warned me about. With the naval base so nearby, there is an unending parade of handsome, eligible bachelors coming to the restaurant every night, often trying to hit on me. And I turn my back on each one of them, not giving them a half a chance. Jimmy sure seemed different than the others, but I've got too much history to give another sailor my heart. Mother would kill me anyways, and I'd just be setting myself up for another fall. "We've been down this road a few other times, young lady," she'd slur. I tried to warn you, but you never take my word for it. No, you have to go and find out for yourself what creeps they are. Your father was a prime example. He couldn't give two hoots about either one of us, and you know it." Now she staggers over to me and begins to cry. "Don't you think I want a better life for my daughter than what I got? Don't you think I know what's good for you? Why can't you respect your mother enough to listen and take her advice? All we'll ever have is each other, Mary. It's just the way it has to be."

God knows there's enough turmoil in my life already without falling for another US sailor. Haven't there already been signs that this wasn't meant to be? Look at how that crazy Sandy attacked me out of nowhere at work. I thought the maniac was really going to kill me right there in the diner's kitchen. She's got Chet wrapped around her finger.

I have to admit to myself that tonight was wonderful, though. Everything was so perfect, right up to the point that he said those three words—why did he have to go and do that? He looked so handsome and I loved the way he held me so close when we danced. It's been a long time since I felt the arms of a man around me. Oh, what am I going on for? I have to put a stop to this now before I hurt him any worse.

I feel as though I'm being torn apart! My head is pounding, my heart is telling me that this could be my last chance. My only chance to know what love really means. I brush a tear from my eye-I don't know what I should do. Just another… Like mother always… I turn from the window and rush to my room. In the safety of my room I undress and put my pajamas on. I can't wait to fall into bed, hoping to escape life altogether there between the cotton sheets and blankets. I bury my face in my pillow and cry. After a long while, I roll over onto my back and look up at the chipped paint hanging from my ceiling. I wipe my eyes dry and close them tightly, but all I can see is his face. His darling, young, handsome face, smiling that wry, half-smiley smirk with his crystal blue eyes piercing me to the core of my soul. I turn on the radio, hoping it will take my mind off of things, but Elvis is singing "I can't help falling in love with you." But even he cannot sing loud enough to drown out the sound of James's voice, "It's okay, Mary. I love you… I love you…"

****

Meanwhile, Sandy's past sneaked up again in her mind. "Sandra! Her mother shrieked. What would make you do a thing like this?" Paula stared at the hairless Barbie doll in her hand. Sandy stared at the floor. She knew one of her nosy sisters would tell her mom. They were nosy, just plain nosy. "I'm waiting for an answer young lady."

"I'm sorry Mommy. I don't know why I did it. I was mad one day. I didn't think anyone would find out."

"Honestly, Sandy, sometimes I think you just like being mean. I don't know what to do with you. Maybe you want me to throw all your toys and stuffed animals in a garbage bag and send them to the dump!"

"Oh, no Mommy! Please don't! I'm sorry for what I did. I promise that I won't do anything like this again!

"Sorry, huh? You'll be sorry when your father hears what you did."

"Mommy, please don't tell him! I promise that I won't do it again—just don't tell daddy about it," Sandy wailed as she remembered her father's harsh punishments that she'd endured. As she began to hyperventilate, she begged for mercy. "Mommy, please say that you won't tell daddy!"

Still rubbing the hairless Barbie doll, Genevieve Walker walked to the open window, staring toward the neighbor's house. She closed the window and drew the curtains closed. "What is it about you that makes you so destructive? Do you take pleasure in testing me? Sandra, something has got to change." She swung around to face her child who stood rigid with a blank face.

"Come here."

"Please Mommy, no."

"Dammit, I said come here girl."

The girl reluctantly edged closer to her mother. "This time I'm going to settle this matter myself." She grabbed Sandy by the hair, twisting it as she got enough to hold her tight.

"Ow! Mommy, no!" Her cries drew the twins to listen outside the door.

Genevieve Walker pummeled the girl with the doll, striking her head over and over and over again. The hard plastic caused incredible pain as it connected with Sandy's scalp. Later when Sandy was alone, she tried to count the bumps on her head and found nearly a dozen.

"Ahh haa haa awww," the girl moaned in pain with each blow.

"You are going to start treating your things with care and your parents and sisters with respect, starting right now! I've had it with your sarcasm about the twins."

"But Mommy, they make fun of me too." Sandy pleaded.

"This lying is going to stop! Right here, right now! Your sisters have treated you as nicely as anyone can. You make up all these stories about how they've teased you and then you expect me to believe you."

Outside the door, the twins hold their hands over each others' mouths, muffling their laughter.

When the assault with the doll ended, Gen pulled up her daughter's skirt and began a spanking that lasted at least twenty minutes. "Mommmmy stop!" Sandy always thought that her mother's discipline would be softer than her father's. She was wrong.

Her mother grabbed her by the shoulders and turned her as they met face to face. Sandy's face was deep red, covered with tears and her nose had run down to her chin. Genevieve's face was frozen in anger.

"You will stay up here in your room the rest of the night. Without supper. Maybe this will help to make a nice young lady out of you." She walked to the door as the twins scampered away back to their own rooms.

After the door shut, Sandy dried her face and angrily looked around the room at her things. There, on the top shelf in the corner, the yellow bunny she'd been given in her Easter basket months before. She quietly carried it to her bed and snickered as she stabbed it in the back of its neck with a paring knife and held it under her arm as she tried to fall asleep.

****

They sat silently in Mary's cramped, ratty little office as Chet searched for the words to begin. Mary had closed the door behind them when everyone had entered for privacy, but the heat in the tiny room soon became stifling. Lime green paint hung in chips from the ceiling and flaked from the walls. A bulletin board on the wall listed who was scheduled to work each day.

"Mary, is it always this hot in here?" Chet growled.

She nodded. "Yeah, boss. You never got around to having that air conditioner put in that I asked you for two years ago." Chet wiped his forehead with a dingy white handkerchief and pretended to make a mental note to remember to take care of it. Sandy sniffled and cracked her gum.

Finally, Chet organized his thoughts and looked at the two women. "Okay, you two, we're gonna get to the bottom of what happened. I want to hear from you both why you had your little scuffle in the kitchen."

"Who's gonna start?" Stillness filled the sauna-like office and Sandy shifted nervously in her seat. Mary frowned at Chet and found an interesting spot on the ceiling to study.

"Come on ladies, no one is leavin' this room until we get this settled. You're two of the best, but I can't have these catfights going on when I've got a restaurant to run. If me and Tommy hadn't shown up, you mighta killed each other." Sandy shot a nervous glance at Mary, sat up straighter in her chair and composed herself. She began wringing her hands as she spoke.

"Well Chet, you see, I would have been willing to forgive and forget about the whole thing, if you and Tom hadn't come in when you did. Maybe it's lucky for me that you did, but I don't want to make no trouble; I come in here to do my job and just try to get along with everybody." Mary's eyes stared icily, fixed on the other woman.

Sandy's hands began shaking as she reached for a tissue from her pocketbook. "I guess you might say this is all my fault, I admit it. I was hurrying back in after having bussed table number four, with a huge tray of dishes and glass, and you know, stuff." Her eyes grew wide with drama. "Just then, Mary here came bustin' out of the door with her order and I got startled and clumsy, and one of the dirty plates slid off my tray and spilled onto her clothes."

Sandy continued her version of the story. "Well of course, you know me Chet, I went to apologizing and grabbed a rag real quick and started to clean off her up, but she shrieked at me and pushed me away, calling me a stupid klutz, a ninny, and that I should watch where I was going, and be more careful; you know, stuff like that. I said Jeeze Mary— I'm so sorry, I didn't mean to make you so sore at me. It was an accident."

Sandy sniffled and held the hanky to her nose. "But she kept insulting me, saying I should find a job where I didn't have to think and walk at the same time, you know how sarcastic she can be."

Sandy gave a wounded look to Mary. She began to sniffle and dabbed the tears in her eyes with a tissue. "I got down on my hands and knees and tried to wipe her shoe again, saying over and over, 'I'm sorry, I'm sorry,' but she sat down her tray and hauled off and slapped me real hard, right here on my left cheek." She pointed to her cheek and winced as though the faintest touch still caused pain. "I even offered to buy her a new work outfit. That's when she really got mad and said, 'Whattaya think I am, a charity case, need you to buy me clothes?' She shoved me away so hard that I landed in the garbage and my uniform was covered with the stinky stuff."

To Mary's astonishment, a current of tears actually began running down Sandy's cheeks and dripped onto her lap. "I tried to get back up, but she just kept pushing me back down, saying that that's where I belonged, in the trash. I said 'Mary, I didn't mean to do it, we gotta get back to work. We have customers waiting.'"

This brought a sympathetic nod from Chet. "That's when she really decked me one and the room went black. Next thing I remember is you and Tommy standing over me." She held her handkerchief over her nose and mouth, tears flowing and her body quaking with emotion. Chet went to her, and kneeling beside her, patted her shoulder. He of course was falling for Sandy's whole fabrication of the facts.

"Now, now, Sandy. It's all right. It's all over now, try to get a hold of yourself." He stared icily at Mary, "What do you have to say about all this?" Mary just stared at him, infuriated by Sandy's performance, and frustrated that he would believe her.

"My God, woman, look what you've done to her. Don't you have anything to say for yourself? You may have been with me for over five years, but that doesn't give you the right to go around clobbering the other waitresses. For a manager you sure have a crappy way of handling the other employees sometimes. I've had it with you, Mary-this isn't the first time you've picked on one of the other girls."

Chet leveled with them. "You both know that you two are a couple of my best waitresses, you work hard, and the customers like you. "Mary, you've managed this place for a long time and you've done a very good job."

Chet patted Sandy's shoulder as he glared at Mary. "But I don't want to see this happen again, Missy, do you get me? One more time and you're out of here-everybody else gets along real good except for you. You're always in the middle of somethin'. You have to start handling the wait staff better than this. Now I want you to apologize." Mary scowled at him and tried to form the words in her mouth but they wouldn't come. "I mean it, Mary you apologize to Sandy right here and now or you're outta here right now!" Mary swallowed hard but she lacked the flair for Sandy's sinister, dramatic acting. "Mary!"

"I'm sorry." She stared at the floor. Sandy nodded and looked at Chet who had to turn the knife just a little more.

"Speak up, Mary. I didn't hear what you said. I want to make sure I heard you right." She looked up at the ceiling and shrugged.

"I said I'm sorry Sandy." Chet lifted Sandy's head with her chin but she still had that pitiable look on her face and tears on her cheeks.

"See, she's sorry. Now that's more like it, but listen and listen good, Mary-if you can't get along with the other girls here, you're gonna have to go. This is your last warning. I can't have good waitresses quitting just because you've been bullying them, so this is it, girl, am I makin' myself clear Mary?" She stared him down.

"Perfectly clear, Chet. Can I go?"

"Yeah, get back to work. Sandy, you okay to work tonight? I can call Maria in if you want to go home." She held her handkerchief to her forehead to calm her feigned headache.

Sandy rubbed her temples. "No, Chet, I can work. As long as I know there isn't gonna be any more trouble. Besides, I need the money. Mary, do you have an aspirin in here, my head is splittin' from all this."

"There's not gonna be any trouble again, right Mary?" Chet snorted.

"Yeah, right." Mary dispensed the aspirin from her desk drawer and exited the stuffy office.

Chet murmured after her, "Like I said kid, one more screw up and you're outta here."

Chet breathed easier when they were closing the place for the night without further incident. Naturally the whole staff was aware of the problem between Mary and Sandy by now. Even Tony the bartender commented on how well they seemed to be getting along again. It was another hectic night at the Chesapeake Crab House, but Mary couldn't stop looking for James. She hoped to see him, yet she hoped not to. She couldn't remember any other guy ever affecting her this way-and she wasn't too keen on it. At long last, the shift ended without a sign of Seaman Gallant. Both disappointed and relieved, Mary went home.

Chapter 3

It was 7 a.m. when the phone beside Mary's bed began ringing. She tried to ignore it, stuffing her pillow over her head. After a few minutes, it stopped, and then it started in again. She picked up the receiver and answered, "Hello?"

"Hi, is this Mary?" He really couldn't be sure.

"Yeah, it is."

"This is Jimmy Gallant. I was hoping that we could get together sometime today."

She covered a yawn with her hand and asked, "What time is it?"

"I've got about five minutes past seven."

"Man, you sailors are early risers, aren't you?"

Jimmy laughed and asked, "So how about it, gorgeous? Let's just go down to the beach for a quiet walk." They decided where and when and she leapt out of bed to get ready.

At the beach, they walked in the warm sand, carrying their shoes. When he made an attempt to hold her hand, she slipped hers away and shook her head. They found an empty bench and sat down. He could see that she was about to break things off with him, just by the blank, distant looks she gave him. The gulls cried and fluttered around the fishermen's lines.

She began: "How can I begin to tell you how sorry I am for letting things get so out of control? I never should have accepted your invitation for dinner. I made an awful mistake, and now it's you who has to pay.

I realized too late that I was wading into water that was deeper than I was comfortable in. That was the main problem; I wanted you so much, but I'm not the right girl for you, Jimmy. The only thing I can think of to make things right is to tell you my whole story. I feel safe telling you this, knowing that I can trust you with the truth. I knew it the first few moments of our date the other night. You have a right to know the whole story, after the way I've led you on."

"Mary, you never 'lead me on.'" He smiled as he told her.

"You'll remember that I said I never knew my father. I didn't come right out and say it, but you can probably guess that he was a sailor, too. That along with a few unfortunate experiences I've had with relationships with sailors and other men is why I gave up trying to find romance in my life. It's nothing personal with you. Please believe that. Jimmy, since I met you I've never been more happy. He tried to put his arm around her but she shrugged him off again.

"Please don't." she said. "When my mother's parents found out that she was 'in trouble,' they sent her away to live with her Aunt Rosie in Virginia Beach. Rosie was a kind, compassionate widow who treated my mother very well, like a daughter. Barely making ends meet even before my mother arrived, Rosie assured her that things would work out all right and that we would manage."

Mary's voice choked with emotion. "After living off her husband's pension for four years, she had to take a job at the neighborhood supermarket bagging groceries for extra money when mother arrived. Mom tried to locate my father through the Navy, but being as they weren't legally married, they informed her that they were under no obligation to supply her with information regarding him. She called them back for months before becoming bitter and giving up.

I always blamed my mother for our hardships as I was growing up, until one day when Rosie sat me down and went through the whole

THEY NEVER REALLY LEAVE

story with me. There was a lot that mother had never told me. I guess I was about twelve at the time, and Rosie was eighty-five. She was eighty-seven when she passed away. She explained how heartsick my mother was and how mom started drinking a lot a few months after I'd been born, partly from her broken heart, partly due to the pressure of holding down two full-time jobs plus taking in laundry to provide for her and me." Mary pulled strands of her crimson hair back from her face, leaning forward to hug her knees.

Jimmy'd had a lump in his throat when Mary started. Now he felt like he was suffocating. "Sweetheart, I know how hard it is living with an alcoholic." Jimmy shrugged his shoulders. "There are things I remember from my childhood that I'll never be able to forget," he said.

She brushed his cheek with the back of her hand. "I know, but please, Jimmy—don't interrupt or I'll never make it through telling you this." For one bittersweet moment, she held his face in her hands, leaned over, and kissed him. "Alcohol became mom's escape from everything. Along with the alcohol came droves of low-life men to call on my mom. I guess she thought she needed them to feel wanted, if for just for a night. To see her now, you wouldn't believe that at one time she was quite beautiful. Rosie must have had a lot of patience, as it fell on her many times to care for me while my mother either was drunk or out at some man's apartment. Although mom never missed a day of work at her jobs, all she did when not working was drink. Rosie told me of the many nights she'd sat up with my mother, when she came home drunk and crying, trying to console her. Mom started drinking to deaden her feelings, but it sometimes magnified the pain and she would cry for hours on my aunt's shoulder."

Mary took James by the arm and led him to the rail along the pier. They both looked out over the expanse of the Atlantic Ocean. He saw the far-away look in her eyes, as though she wished that she wouldn't have to go on. "Jimmy, I'm not telling you these things to make you feel sorry for me. I do not need or want your sympathy. I just want you to understand, so that you can forget about me and go on with your life."

"I didn't understand why my Mom did the things she did when I was a child." Rosie told me that my mother loved me in her own way. Her heart had been broken when she realized the sailor that had been the first man she ever gave herself to was never returning to us, was never going to come back and take care of us and make us a real family. Most times when I come home from work to find her passed out on the couch, I just feel sad for her, thinking how abandoned she must have felt back then. The hopelessness. I wonder if I wouldn't have turned to the bottle as she had, if I were in her shoes. That's why I'm so hesitant to let a relationship start with a man-I can see what can happen. I don't want to become my mother, Jimmy."

"Baby, I would never do that to you," he said.

"I wish I could believe that, hon. I just have so many questions and doubts scrambling around inside my head right now. I feel like I'm goin' nuts, really."

They walked back along the pier for a while. "Aunt Rosie was the only family my mom had left that would have anything to do with her. They talked once about having me adopted, but it was a hard thing for either of them to discuss, and my mom would always end up crying and wrapping her arms around her swollen belly. She couldn't bear the thought of giving her child away, Rosie said.

My mom kept working right up through her eighth month of pregnancy. One day she came home exhausted and in tears. "I just can't do this anymore Rosie," she said. "All I do is worry all day at work, and then lay awake worrying at night. I'm so tired right now I could just die. I'm not going to be a good mother, and my baby's going to grow up in poverty and hate me." Her aunt tried to console her, holding her tightly and rocking her.

"Now, now Margie. You just worry too much. We're going to get by-it'll all come out in the wash," Rosie said. That was one of her pet expressions.

"But I'm only eighteen. What do I have to offer a child?"

"Why, you'll have a home, enough to eat, and a family to love your baby. The three of us will be a family, you'll see."

"Love?" my mother snapped back. "How is love going to fill my baby's empty stomach? You can't afford to have the two of us living here, let alone another mouth to feed! You barely got by even before I came to live with you, and there isn't room here for a baby besides." Her face went blank. "I have to give it up. It's the only way." She was crying and rubbing her tummy. "This baby should have the right to live a good life, not the one I can give it. It's the right thing to do, Rosie, we both know it is. I'm beat Rosie and I need to go in and lay down." She stood to leave. "Tomorrow after work, I'm going to that adoption agency we saw in the paper."

Aunt Rosie gently pushed my mother back down in her chair. She looked her square in the eye and said, "Margie Bauer, I've known you since you were just a baby cooing in your mother's arms. And if you're sure that you can spend the rest of your life never knowing your own child, never getting to watch it grow up, wondering what she or he looks like on each birthday and on the holidays, then you just go on and do what you think you need to do." Her eyes narrowed. "If you really think it's so easy just to give your baby up to strangers, then you're not the person I thought you were, and I'm very, very disappointed in you."

"Rosie was a really good person. She meant the world to my Mom. But she had heard enough of this adoption stuff one Friday when my mom came home from work.

"Damn it girl, I love you. And because I do, I love that little baby that's in your belly. It's part of you, and it's part of me now, too. I can't for the life of me understand why you should give up so easily. We might be eatin' a lot of pork 'n beans for a while, but by God, if you go and adopt that child out, you're gonna regret it every day of your life, and I will too. We'll get by, child. Most importantly, this baby will grow up knowing that her mother loved her enough to keep her, no matter the cost. You just imagine what it would be like to grow up never knowing your own mother. You really think it'll be better off with strangers? Well if you do, young lady, then you go ahead and let them take it."

She threw her hands up in the air. "I wash my hands of the whole thing. I've said what I intended to say."

"It's best for my baby," mother cried as she stood to her feet and hurried to her room, slamming the door behind her.

The next night my mom returned home from work with a huge grin on her face. Rosie read what it meant right away, and said, "Oh, I do love you, kiddo. And we're gonna be just fine! You wait and see." They ate their supper and afterward busied themselves clearing out the back sun porch for a nursery.

Well, I guess they did eat a lot of pork 'n beans after I was born, and somehow they got by. That's when my mom started drinking, as I said, just a couple months after I was born. She spent a lot of time at the bar down the street and in strange men's apartments, still searching for the love and acceptance she'd never gotten from my father. I'll never know how Rosie made it through all that. I asked her one time and she just laughed and said, "What else was I going to do? You're family."

"Later that same year, my mother became pregnant again. She was only into her first few months when she collapsed at work and was taken to the emergency room. She had what they call a "tubal pregnancy," so the doctors had to do surgery and she lost the baby."

Mary pulled a tissue from her pocketbook, just in case the tears started. I remember some happy times while I was growing up, but mostly feeling very confused and hurt by mother's drinking. For a long time, I thought it was my fault, that she hated me and was sorry for keeping me, until Rosie set the record straight, that is.

I was fourteen when Rosie died. It was the worst time of my life. I'll never forget standing there looking at her in the casket, realizing that I'd never have her to turn to again. After the funeral, I stayed in my room reading with the door locked, as much as possible, and only came out to make something to eat or go to the bathroom. I tried to only come out after I knew she'd left the house, so that I could straighten things up a little. It was horrible. There would be crushed beer cans strewn about the floor and overflowing ashtrays, some that had been knocked to the floor, littering it with cigarette butts that took me hours to pick up. There was crushed pretzels and popcorn ground into the carpet in the living room. The whole house was beginning to smell like a garbage dump." Mary shook her head as she continued, "There were even times when some man would still be sprawled out on the couch when I got up."

Within a week, the truant officer started coming around and

knocking on the door. It didn't take him long to locate her at work, and the day he did, she came home very late and drunk and not alone. She banged on my door."

"Open up, Mary. I said open this damned door up! You crazy kid, you got the truant officer coming after me at work now. Mary! You better open this door up right now!" Her voice slurred as she said "I'm not puttin' up with this anymore! Open up!" I heard whispering outside my bedroom door and then suddenly, crash! The door came off its hinges and a huge hulk of a man stepped inside, holding out his arm for my mother to enter. She staggered in, came over to me and slapped me hard across the face, knocking my book out of my hands. "You little brat. You're gonna start listening to me, and you're going back to school-tomorrow. Things are gonna be different around here from now on, girlie. I can't go gettin' fired because you keep skipping school." She and the hulk stormed back out of my room, leaving the broken door lay on my bedroom floor.

Later on that night, Jake, the guy who kicked in my door, put it back on the hinges but removed the lock. All night long I could hear the two of them out there laughing and carrying on. It terrified and sickened me to know that I no longer had the security of locking my door. She could come in anytime now and rant at me for hours on end. And she did just that. I hated her-I hated my life, and I missed Rosie terribly. I hated the constant stream of my mother's men friends who'd come over, drink with her, and end up spending the night. I remember thinking that eventually the world would run out of new men, but they just kept coming, uglier, meaner and drunker all the time.

My so-called life went on, and just when I thought things couldn't get any worse at home, they did.

Mary took a deep breath and exhaled slowly. Her eyes began shifting between Jimmy and then to the water below them. "This is very difficult to tell you, Jimmy. You're the only living soul I've ever told, and I have to get through it as fast as I can before I change my mind!" She pounded the weatherworn railing of the pier as she tried to regain her composure.

Tears streamed down her cheeks as she spoke. "When I was fifteen, one night I awoke, hearing the floor creak in my room and realized that someone else was there. I saw only a shadow, but when I sat up in bed, the person grabbed me and held his hand over my mouth. He held me down and raped me.

Where did she find such a ruthless, unfeeling man? If it was love she was looking for, these scoundrels weren't the type to get it from—I never knew what the next night would bring."

Jimmy tried to hold her in his arms and love away the pain, but she again pushed him away. She didn't need a lover right now. She just needed him to listen.

I never told my mother what that man did to me. I realized that she didn't have a clue as to what happened. And that's the way I intend to always leave it. She's got a pretty steady boyfriend now, Frankie, and he's fat and smells but at least he's never tried anything with me. They sit and watch t.v. each night, drinking themselves into oblivion."

Mary finally reached over and held Jim's hand in hers. "Man, this is harder than I even imagined it would be."

Jimmy answered, "Mary, I'm in love with you and nothing from your past is going to change that."

Jimmy, I've had very few relationships with men, as you can imagine. A few times, I decided to date sailors and it always ended up in disaster. I've dated men who were civilians and they have burned me too. So yes, I'm bitter. And I'm perfectly comfortable with the thought of spending the rest of my life alone. I don't need a man in order to be 'complete.'"

She went on—after the last guy I dated I swore off men and I've never trusted one since. She searched for understanding in his eyes and found it.

"Please don't take anything I've said personally. You seem like a really nice guy and I enjoyed what we had of our evening together. But now that you know my past, I'm sure you'll understand me when I say that this relationship will go nowhere. You deserve a lot better, and a girl who will treat you nice and with respect."

"No, Mary. You're the only girl I want." He fought back tears. Can't you understand that I'm in love with you? I want to spend the rest of my life with you. Please, Mary."

She shook her head. "In a moment, I'm going to turn and walk away. I'm asking you to let me go—don't follow me and please don't come to my house anymore. Thank you for your company the other night, but I'm asking you, please don't come around me again. I don't know how else to put it. I can't have you thinking that we could have a future together-there's just no way, Jimmy. Please forget about me and go find a nice girl who'll make a proper wife for you and a good mother for your children."

"Mary, please don't do this. I love you!" His voice choked with emotion.

"Oh, and don't come around the restaurant-I already almost lost my job because of you." She looked down and walked away from him.

I watched Mary walk away until she was just a spot on the beach and then she was gone. Damn! As I thought about her mother's problems and her nightmarish teenage years, everything I'd seen and known of Mary finally made sense. That she didn't end up at an insane asylum, after what she'd been through was a miracle.

I stood there with this sickening feeling in my stomach. I felt guilty for every moment of my life that I'd indulged myself in self-pity for my own home life. It hurt to think that she expected me to be shallow and undependable, like the other guys that she'd gone out with. I'm ashamed to remember the harsh things I thought about her when I first met her.

The beautiful scent of her perfume still lingered on my t-shirt. I inhaled deeply, wishing she were still sitting here beside me. I scooped up a handful of sand and let it sift through one hand into the other and then back to the ground.

I'm a big dope to let her walk away from me. Oh, Mary, how can I convince you to trust me? I only have three weeks before shipping out now, who knows what'll happen over there and if I'll ever get to see you again. No, I can't think that way. I love her and I have to figure out a way to make her understand.

She has no idea how much I care for her-she thinks I'm just like all the other men who have breezed in and out of her life, using her for a doormat. She'll never know me in any other way until I can talk her into spending more time with me, getting to know me. So there it is! I have to convince her to go out with me again. But how?

Suppose I drive over, have a little talk with her mother, and explain my feelings for Mary. What's the worst she could do-throw me out of her house? I feel like it's my only option. Oh, man. Her mom hates sailors too.

"Well hello there, you cute sailor!" The attractive woman on my right says as she removes her sunglasses. It's that other waitress from the diner, and she scoots right in next to me on the bench. "What's a handsome man like you doing sittin' alone out here all alone on such a beautiful day?"

I try to stay polite, but I don't feel like talking right now. Not with her, anyways.

"Some days I come down to the pier because I like to watch the fishermen reel 'em in. But I've been here a while now, so I guess I'll be going—"

"Don't be silly! I just got here to rescue you from the throes of loneliness!" she said theatrically as she pulls me back down on the bench. "Ooooh! What strong shoulders you have honey." I sit there kind of out of it still and she puts her arm around me, massaging my neck, then my shoulders and my upper back.

"That really feels great, but like I said, I was just leaving," I say.

"What was your name again?" she asks, undaunted.

"Jimmy."

"Well come on, Jimmy, I'll walk with you to your car." She just won't quit. Oh no. I'm beginning to see how Mary felt when I was trying to court her. This girl gives me the creeps. She's so forward, and makes no bones over showing it. I stand to walk away and she looks like I just stabbed her in the heart.

"Jimmy—from the moment I laid eyes on you I knew that you might be my Mr. Right." She springs off the bed.

I pretend that I don't hear that. "I'm really sorry. I've forgotten your name too."

"It's Sandy, honey," she said as she slipped her arm around mine and slides her sunglasses back on as we make our way down the pier.

She really is very pretty, dressed in blue capri shorts and white lacy sleeveless top. Her auburn hair shimmers in the morning sun. But she's not Mary.

When we reach the lot where my car is parked, I begin to lead Sandy up there.

"Oh, Jimmy. What's the hurry to leave? Can't we walk for awhile. Hmm?"

"Yeah, it's a beautiful day but I have something that I have to do. It's been nice talking to you, Sandy." I can't peel her from my arm. It's 11:45. Mary goes in to work at 1 p.m. and she's all I can think about.

"C'mon, please? Say, there's a nice little bar just another three or four blocks down. I'm thirsty. Are you thirsty?" She could have been kin to a parrot the way she talks. "How about a couple drinks before we end our lovely morning together?"

"Look," I say. "There's someone special in my life right now and I don't want to mess up." I shake her arm from me and her sunglasses fall to the sand. She quickly picked them back up and shook the sand out of them. "Get a clue, will ya? I've tried to be nice to you, but I love another girl."

Sandy's eyes narrowed and her temper flared. "I know all about it. It's that Mary from work. Didn't you understand when I told you that she doesn't go for men? Let me ask you, why isn't she here walking arm in arm with you today?"

"You lied to me. She has a problem trusting men, but she's not a lesbian. Why would you lie to me about something like that?" Sandy removed her sunglasses and looked me straight in the eye.

"I would never lie to you, Sugar. She hasn't had a date for the two years I've been working with her, I know that much for sure. Besides that, you ought to have heard how she was talking you down the other night and the names she was calling you. You haven't got a chance with her, Jimmy."

I stepped out of the way of a jogger coming down the beach and replied, "You know what, Sandy? It's none of your business. You and

I don't even know each other."

"C'mon, Jimmy. Just a couple drinks. Where's the fire at that you have to run off after anyhow?" She was relentless, and a couple beers did sound good—it was probably eighty degrees out here in the sun.

I swung around to walk up the beach with her as she grinned. She tried to take my arm again but this time I resisted and she just shrugged and kept on walking beside me. The beers did a world of good for my disposition, and before long I was sitting there seeing a whole lot more of Sandy and less of Mary.

****

The sound of a motorcycle stirred me awake. I sat up on the edge of the bed and couldn't believe that Sandy was there. I just shook my head and agonized there for a long time before Sandy whispered, "Good morning, hero. Did you enjoy last night as much as I did?" She tried to pull me back down but I resisted her.

I didn't answer her. She and I both knew that she'd set me up. But what would Mary think when she finds out? Oh, God help me. I can't believe this. When I recover from shock, I quickly put my clothes on.

Sandy calls out to me, "Jimmy, please stay with me. I don't want to be alone."

I say, "Then go out and find another guy to get him drunk so he does something he'll regret for the rest of his life."

She throws a shoe at me. "Damn men—you're all alike! Go on then."

It should take me about twenty minutes in traffic to get to Mary's mom's house, who knows, I might luck out and catch her sober. I've got to try it.

****

As I drove, I rehearsed my introduction to Mary's mom. "Good Afternoon, Mrs. Bauer! Now, you don't know me, but your daughter Mary and I met at the restaurant where she works. I really like your daughter, and we've had a little misunderstanding. I was hoping you could help me out." No, she's probably heard that one before. "Good afternoon, Mrs. Bauer! My, you look really nice today. I can see whom your daughter Mary gets her looks from. Speaking of your daughter, Mary…" No, that would sound fresh. "Hi, Mrs. Bauer? My name is James Gallant and I met your daughter Mary at the Chesapeake Crab House one evening. I'm sorry to bother you, m'am, but we've had a little misunderstanding and I was hoping that you could help me get things straightened out with her." Well, that could work. (All right, it's better than, "Hi Mrs. Bauer, I'm a sailor on the Forrestal. And guess what-I'm in love with your daughter Mary! Isn't that just great?")

I scale the rickety wooden stairway up to entrance to the house, pull open the rusty screen door that hangs literally by a thread on its hinges and knock on the warped, peeling door behind it. Paint chips drop like snowflakes and the glass rattles so that I'm afraid it might fall in should I knock any harder. There's no answer at the door, so lean closer and try to peep through a crack in the curtains. Before I can knock again, the curtains are swept back and an annoyed, wrinkled face with dark circles under her eyes peeks through, startling us both. "Ahhhhhhr!" We both screamed. The curtains are pulled across the window again and I can hear cursing on the other side of the door. I try to talk through the door.

"Uh, Mrs. Bauer, could I please have a word with you?" I thought I sounded sincere and non-threatening.

"We ain't buyin' anything or the check's in the mail. Get the hell outta here-you almost scared me to death."

"I'm not selling anything, really. If you'll just open the door up I can explain why I'm here." There's a stream of profanity on the other side of the door again.

"Hey, buddy, what kinda nut are you? Old ladies don't just open their doors to strangers these days. Take off!"

"Oh, of course, I realize that m'am. You can't be too careful these days. But I'm not selling anything, I'm not a bill collector, and I'm not a nut, I just need to talk to you for a few minutes." I wait, but there's no reply. Instead I hear the sound of something heavy striking the floor inside.

"You hear that? That's my 'enforcer.' I got a ball bat in here that'll split your head open if you don't beat it. Now get lost before I call the cops." It seems as though our shouting match on either side of the door has reached a stalemate, then…

"Mrs. Bauer, I'm here to talk to you about your daughter Mary."

"Mary? What's wrong with Mary? Is she all right-she just left for work not twenty minutes ago."

"No, m'am, nothing is wrong with her. She's fine, but I need to talk to you about her." A bloodshot eye peers through the curtain from the other side.

"What do you have to do with my Mary?"

"I'm a friend," I replied.

"Oh, bull. Mary ain't got no friends. I'm her only friend. Everybody else hates her, she told me so herself. Now you better vamoose."

"If you'll just let me in for a few minutes, I can explain everything. Otherwise, I'm going to park myself here on this stoop all night until she comes home."

"Look, you I told you I'd call the cops. I'm reaching for the phone right now…"

"You wouldn't turn in a man to the cops who was in love with your daughter, would you? Mrs. Bauer, I—"

"What's this you say you're in love with my Mary? How do you even know her?" she demanded.

"I met her at the Chesapeake Crab House where she works a few nights ago," I said.

"Is that right? Well that don't tell me jack shit about you, buddy. That don't mean you're not some kinda weirdo pervert."

"We've been on a date together, too." I was making progress. I heard the lock being disengaged and she stuck her twisted, wrinkled face out the door.

"A date? Mary never told me about no date. She tells me everything." Her brow furrowed and her eyes were suspicious, looking me up and down.

"Please, Mrs. Bauer. If you'll just let me in, I'll tell you the whole story. I really need your help. Just look at me, do I look like a crazed maniac?" Finally, she pushed the door open and motioned me in, still gripping the aged Louisville Slugger protecting herself.

"If you try anything smart, kid, I'll crack your head open with this here bat."

"Don't worry about that," I said, eyeing the heavy wooden weapon.

"Come on in the front room-I wasn't expectin' no one, so the place isn't picked up like it normally is. Over there—" she pointed with the bat. "You sit on the couch." I take a seat on the worn-out lumpy red sofa against the wall and she lowers herself into a thread-bare, sunken gray seat that had cigarette burns across the arms of it. The end table beside her chair was rustic, looked homemade, with an old lamp with a tilted shade and an overflowing ashtray on it. She lights a cigarette and watches me sweep newspapers and dog-eared magazines aside to make room for me to sit on the couch.

"Nice place you have here," I lied.

"Well it sure ain't the Taj Mahal, but it's home. Now, what's all this about you and Mary goin' on a date and she don't even tell her own Ma?" I clear my throat and try to sit up straight which is impossible because the springs in the sofa, if there ever were any are shot, and I'm sunk down in a huge dip that pins my elbows to my sides. She still studies me like I'm a zoo animal on the other side of the glass. She coughs violently and flicks an ash from her cigarette. "You don't smoke, do ya kid?"

"No m'am, I don't"

"Well, don't you ever start, 'cause it's hell giving them up when you get hooked on 'em. I should know, I've been smokin' for over forty years now." She wasn't a homely woman. I mean, her hair was salt and pepper gray, looking like it hasn't been brushed since yesterday, and the years had wrinkled and puckered her skin. Even with the dark circles that had permanently etched themselves beneath her eyes, you could tell that she used to be pretty. She was dressed in a light blue chambray house dress with a matching belt that encircled her waist. Couldn't be more than five-foot-three, maybe ninety-eight pounds soakin' wet. Mary didn't inherit her height or build from her mother.

She had the telling tic of an alcoholic, just like my dad. I sat there silent for a few moments, still dazed at the appearance of the home and surprised that she finally let me inside.

"Well, don't just sit there, boy-tell me what you want." Mary did inherit her mother's bluntness. I look up from the ragged, patchy black shag rug on the floor and I am stumped on where to start.

I tried to push myself up out of my burrow. "I don't exactly know where to begin." The old woman didn't really intimidate me, aside from the Louisville Slugger she held across her lap, but I knew so much about her and Mary's lives that I had to be careful about what I said. If anything should slip out about the sexual abuse, I could forget about ever being with Mary. How can I tell her that I'm a sailor? Does she really need to know that right now? The bat lay there across her lap, as though taunting me and daring me to give it cause to crack my skull open.

She took a long puff on her cigarette and shook her head. "Well, just start at the beginning. Start in the middle. Hell, I don't care. Just start talkin' or get out. I'm not gonna sit here lookin' at you all night. You are a nice lookin' fella, though."

"Thank you," I said.

"You the same age as Mary?" she asked.

"No, I was going to get to that, I'm twenty-four."

She doubled over laughing and had a smoker's coughing fit at the same time.

"Twenty-four? Lord, boy, you're six years younger than her, d'you know that?"

"I know it—"

"Never thought Mary'd be one to be robbin' the cradle..."

"M'am, I'm hardly in a cradle, and six years is—"

"Twenty-four, huh? Well, I'll be damned!" She laughed and slapped her leg and started getting my dander up.

"Anyway, Mrs. Bauer, now that we've gotten that out of the way—" She sat up straighter in her chair and leaned forward toward me.

"You met her at the Crab House, huh?" Suddenly she became very animated and interested in finding out everything about me. She asked about my family, where they lived, but when she started to ask why I was in Virginia, I stopped her.

"With all due respect, m'am, that's not what I'm here to talk to you about. I'm really crazy about Mary, and I think she likes me too, but—"

"But what?"

"I guess I better tell you the whole story of how we met in order to explain. I proceeded to describe my fateful first meeting with Mary, the collapsing table, the flames, the fire extinguisher, everything. Her eyes sparkled and she slapped the arm of her chair, laughing raucously and going into another coughing fit. This was embarrassing, but I had to tell her everything in order to get across the importance of my visit today. I went on to tell her about the second time I went to the restaurant, and how Mary had disappeared early that night. The woman nodded in understanding.

"Yeah, she looked pretty ragged one night when she came home. I could tell that she'd been in a tussle with one of those girls again. They're always pickin' on her, you know. She never starts fights, but I brought up my girl not to take crap from nobody, and she always gets blamed for everything that happens in that dump." She butted the cigarette in the ashtray and coughed again.

I told her about the night I came by here and finally convinced Mary to go out with me. I told her how we met at the restaurant, and what a nice time we had. Everything was perfect, I said, until I told Mary that I loved her. She lit another cigarette and leaned on one elbow in the chair, looking at me inquisitively for what seemed to be an hour.

"What happened after that?" she asked, smirking at me.

"She got upset. She told me not to say that. She went to the ladies' room and ducked out a side door and left. Next day I get a "Dear John" letter from her telling me to stay away from her and the diner." I think I've finally broken through the woman's tough exterior to stir her maternal instincts, and she nods, almost sympathetically. She rubbed and fingered the baseball bat that lay across her lap. When she finally did speak, her voice was softer. Softer, and more compassionate.

"Well, Jimmy. You did say your name is Jimmy, right?" I nodded. "Mary has had a few boyfriends over the years-not a great many, you understand, but she always ends up gettin' shafted in the end, if you know what I mean. Takes after me, that way. One of 'em even got her to lend him a whole bunch of money, five hundred dollars, I think. Met her one more time after that to tell her that he was bringin' the money over that night, and then he disappeared outta town. She never got a dime of it back. And, she's gone out with a couple of those damned sailors from the base, pardon my French, and like I told her she would, got burned again every time. I tried the best I could to warn her, but Mary's got a real stubborn streak in her. She gets her mind to doin' somethin' and there's nothin' gonna stop her." I nodded. "I think she finally did get smart about dating those no-account Navy guys, because her life has been real nice and settled for some time now." She edged forward in her chair took a long drag on her smoke. "So what are you, a student over there at that university?" She was pinning me down with the question, and I was sweating up a storm and I'd feel a lot more credible and convincing if I wasn't pinned down in this pitiful sink-hole of a couch, looking so vulnerable and small.

"I think Mary's the best waitress there is at the Crab House." I had to divert her attention away from these questions for a bit longer-I wasn't ready to own up to the truth. I was beginning to wonder if I ever would be ready.

"Well, yes, I'm sure she is. She's always been a hard worker, Mary. Truth is, I've never actually been down there, but my Frankie has. He said it was real nice. But she comes home dead-tired every night, I know that much. Places like that don't appreciate it when they got good help, you know. They're always tryin' to either cut her hours or get her to work double shifts when someone calls in sick. She could do better, but she's never really looked for another job anywhere. Waitress'n is about all she knows. Now, what were we talkin' about?"

"About Mary being a good waitress."

"No, confound it, before that." I shook my head and looked as puzzled as I could, but she was going to squeeze the truth out of me eventually, I could see that. She sighed and took another drag on her cigarette, then snuffed it out in the ashtray as she remembered and slapped herself on the forehead. Oh yeah, now I know. I was just askin' if you're a student over there at that Old Dominion University. Is that how you found your way down here?" My meter had just run out.

"Mrs. Bauer, the truth is," I swallowed hard and couldn't look her in the eyes. "The truth is that I'm stationed on the USS Forrestal." I barely had the words out of my mouth before she jumped to her feet with the dexterity of someone half her age and came at me with the bat.

She gave me an upper cut that was going to leave a black eye for days. How was I gonna explain that to the guys?

"You what? Out! You get outta here, you dirty sonofa..." I struggled out of my hole in the couch as she chased me around the room.

"Mrs. Bauer, I know how you feel about sailors, but you've gotta help me make Mary believe that I'm different from those other ones." I was ducking and zigzagging around the furniture in the room as she swung at me. The tone of her voice had gone from soft to murderous in a moment's time, and her cursing surprised even me.

"I'll help you land in the hospital, dammit! You're not a bit different than any of those other losers! Get out of my house," she screamed as she chased me from the living room.

"But Mrs. Bauer-ow!" she connected the bat with my forearm as I held it up to fend off her blows. "Mrs. Bauer, you're not giving me a chance!"

"I'm giving you a chance to get outta here alive, now get!" She swung the bat again and knocked a small lamp on a table to the floor, smashing it. "Now look what you made me do! You had better get lost or I'll crack your damned skull open. I mean it boy!" I believed her.

I made a break for the kitchen door and reached it, just as the Louisville Slugger came hurling through the air. The bat struck me right between the shoulder blades, then smashed through the door's window pane. Believe me, I didn't skip a beat, I made way outta that door and down the stairway.

The demon-woman stood at the top of the landing cussing me and swinging the bat over her head, "And don't you never come back here, kid-and don't you bother my Mary no more neither. She don't need the likes of you messing her life up again. You hear me boy?" I didn't waste time turning to answer her-I was running for my life! I ran to my car, hopped in and sped down the street, leaning forward in my seat and wincing from the aching in my back, which was nothing compared to how it would feel the next day. I looked back as I paused at the stop sign, and could see the wild-eyed lunatic still waving her arms in the air, stomping around on her porch and I was grateful that I couldn't hear the flood of obscenities that were undoubtedly rolling off her tongue.

Chapter 4

Once again, the young sailor from Jamestown, New York has come to where the Atlantic meets the pristine, sandy shore of Virginia for solace, and no person passing him could fathom the depth and the weight of his thoughts. The surf was gentle this morning, at low tide, and cool, salty breakers caressed his bare feet as they made their way to shore, then receded again. The soft, wet rippled sand sunk under the weight of his feet, but his footprints endured for only a moment, as the next wave hurried in to erase them.

It was 6 a.m. on Sunday morning, May 4, 1967; exactly two weeks before the deployment of the USS Forrestal. He remembered everything about their date—how her hair smelled that night, how it felt to have her in his arms, holding her close to him. In just a matter of a few weeks, James Gallant had grown from a twenty-four year old boy to a grown man who was desperately fighting for the love of a woman that couldn't be won.

A flock of pelicans glided high above in formation, headed south as they did every morning. He took a deep breath of the seaside breeze. He barely noticed the others on the beach, passing him as he ambled along, consumed by his thoughts. A very enthusiastic golden retriever stomped through the waves to greet him, soaking his teeshirt and shorts, nearly knocking Jim into the surf. The dog's chagrined master apologized and ordered his pet back, but Jimmy just smiled and patted the dog's head.

Wiping his hands on his shorts, he continued on, thinking how much easier it had been to be strong for someone else all his life, namely his mother, than it was to be strong now for himself. He never wanted anything more than he wanted Mary, and yet he'd never felt more helpless. What was he supposed to do? He'd confessed his love to Mary and her mother, and had been rejected by both, the latter, far more violently. He shook his head as he contemplated—he and Mary seemed to have come from two different worlds. Yet there remained that common thread, of having an alcoholic parent and all the painful memories that came with that. Still, he'd never known anyone who had been so violated, so degraded as Mary had been. He couldn't begin to fathom the depth of her pain, all he knew was that he wanted to become a part of her life and spend the rest of his days making up for it all. He loved her; this fiery, feisty redhead with a love that couldn't be expressed in words and an aching in the very core of his heart and soul for her that could not be eased.

The sun was climbing higher over the sea as James Gallant turned to walk back in the direction of his car. He was numb with hopelessness and grief, except for the throbbing in his upper back where the bat had landed its blow the night before. He rubbed the huge purple bruise on his right forearm from the other strike by the bat.

Jimmy walked up and sat down on the dry sand and looked out at the huge blue expanse before him. Why was he worrying? After Sandy tells Mary what happened there wouldn't be a romance to worry about anyway. How could he have been so stupid?

Climbing back into his car, he closed the door and looked out over the majestic blue ocean, watching the breakers curl and roll their way to shore. He was desperate to make Mary understand how much he loved her. She'd asked him not to go by the restaurant anymore, and going to her house to deal with "Psycho Mama" and her bat didn't sound like such a good idea either. One thing is for sure—Mary probably wants to never see him again now.

Where else could he cause their paths to cross? There must be somewhere that she goes besides work and home. Wait a minute, if her mother seldom leaves the house, Mary must do all the shopping and marketing. There was an old supermarket two blocks down from her house; she might go there for groceries. But on what day? She said her schedule was irregular at the diner, but usually she worked Monday, Tuesday, Thursday, Saturday and Sunday. That leaves Wednesday and Friday. He decided to try Wednesday first. But at what time?

He started his car and drove across town to the market, finding out that it opened at 7 a.m. every day of the week. Mary would probably want to avoid the rush of hungry tourists that arrive daily and inundate the local markets to stock up their rental properties for the week. She'd probably try to get there when it first opened up.

Three days later, he'd traded his mess hall duty for another day so that he could wait in the seedy parking lot of the "Super Shopper Supermarket" at 7 am to see if she showed. He pulled around the side of the building and turned his engine off. From here, he'd have a clear view of the front door and know if and when she went in. 7:05: Maybe she was running late today. He flipped on the radio for some tunes while he waited and the Mamas and the Papas were singing "California Dreamin'." 7:15: Maybe he got her days off wrong. Man! This can't be happening, he thought. The smell of fresh bread baking in the supermarket's bakery wafted through his open window and reminded him that he'd skipped breakfast. Mary, where are you?

In a blur, a red mustang zoomed into a spot four places down from where Jim was parked. There she was! She looked sensuous, he thought, in the red and white sleeveless top and red cutoff shorts that revealed her delicate, slender long legs.

"Carpe diem," he mumbled to himself as he got out and followed her steps into the store. He grabbed the two dozen long-stemmed roses that he purchased from a florist the day before and headed in.

He found her in the canned aisle, and coming up from behind her, he held the flowers behind his back. "Do you need help finding anything, m'am?" he asked. As she was turning to decline the offer, her eyes widened and she glowered at him.

"What're you doin' here?" She put the jar of mayonnaise in her cart. He brought the flowers around and presented them to her. She took the package, hesitantly.

"Wow, Mary. If looks could kill I'd be a dead man," he joked.

She was abrupt. "Dont you dare try to act like nothing happened the other night between you and Sandy. She's been rubbin' my nose in it as often as she gets a chance. Now you've got to understand why I don't date. It's only ever caused me heartache every time. Go on, get away from me. I can't stand the sight of you anymore," she demanded.

"The very same day that you're telling me that I'm the only girl you want, that you're in love with me, you're slippin' between the sheets with one of my biggest enemies. You must have figured out by now that she was setting you up?"

I tried to be candid and honest. "Mary, I take full responsibility for what happened. I got drunk. I drove her back to her place. But when I woke up the next day, she was the last person I expected to be in the bed. It sickens me now—I have absolutely no feelings for her. All I have is shame and remorse. And I hate myself for hurting you."

"Yeah, well one of us was bound to screw this thing up, at least it wasn't me." She threw the roses at his feet. "Go take these to your bimbo Sandy. I should have stopped this a long time ago. No man can be trusted. I was beginning to think you could, but I was just another sucker being burned again." She pushed her way on by him. "I have to get my groceries and get out of here before the pesky tourists start showing up to stock up their rentals."

Jimmy was trying to collect the roses on the floor. "Come on, baby." He stood on the other side of her cart to block her, roses in hand. "You know that we're in love. I don't blame you for one second for being furious with me. I don't deserve your forgiveness but I'm asking for it anyways. All I'm asking for is another date. Please Mary—I've been going nuts ever since the other night. I hate myself."

She pushed her cart free from his grasp, but then leaned against the shelves holding the pasta and sank to the floor, weeping. Jim tried to

THEY NEVER REALLY LEAVE

console her but she pushed him away. He stood there next to her as other customers started arriving. They looked at Jimmy with contempt as they passed by. Before long, the store manager showed up and asked Mary, "Ma'm, is everything all right? Is this guy bothering you? I can escort him from the premises if you'd like."

Mary stood back up and answered, "No, I'm fine. We're breaking up, that's all."

The manager walked away muttering to himself, "What kind of lunkhead would let a beauty like her get away?"

Jimmy was shaking with emotion now. "Is that what we're doing Mary, breaking up?" No answer. "Mary, can't you forgive me? I swear to you that I never did that before and that I will never do it again. There are a lot of things that I've been doing lately that I've never done before."

She dries her tears on a hanky from her pocketbook. "Like what?"

Like falling head-over-heels in love with someone. I've never wanted anything in my whole life like I want you," he replied. "And I've never been beat up by a baseball bat over a girl, either."

"Mary, I love you. It's simple as that. I don't care about the past-it's ancient history. What I care about is you. You gotta believe me. I want to be with you and I want to take care of you. You can forget about all the bad relationships you've had before, because I swear that I'll never, ever hurt you again."

"My mother wanted to beat your brains in, you know."

"And she nearly did. C'mon, Mary, I'll do anything for you to give me a second chance. I'm sick with love for you-I've never wanted anything more in my whole life."

She stood there frozen, in the valley of decision; staring at the roses and then looking back at Jimmy. He knew it was a corny thing to do, but the clerk stocking the shelves down the aisle grinned as Jimmy got down on his knees.

"You-will you get up off the floor? Get up! Come on, really, this is so embarrassing." She looked up and down the aisle to see if anyone was watching and blushed.

"I'm not getting up until you tell me that you'll see me again. Mary, it's less than two weeks before I leave. I can't go without getting this settled. I swear-I'll go crazy!" With one hand she was holding the roses, and with the other she was trying to pull him to a standing position.

"James! This isn't funny! Get up off the floor. I mean it, or I'll-I'll beat you with these flowers!" Instead, he gently drew her down to the floor with him and kissed her. Her arms went around his neck as they kissed again. "Oh, boy are we gonna be in trouble with my mother," she said.

"I don't care, Mary. I love you and I'll do anything for you. I'd face a hundred baseball bats to be with you."

"Don't tell me she got my old Louisville Slugger out after you."

"Oh yeah she did. And she made good use of it, too," he said. She leaned back on her ankles, a hand on his shoulder.

"She didn't hurt you, did she?"

"Not nearly as much as you did when you walked out on me." He caressed her beautiful crimson hair with his hands. "I'm in love with you."

"I know it. I know." Her face went from stormy to placid as she confessed, "I love you too, Jimmy. I can't believe it, I didn't want to believe it, but I really do." They kissed again, to the applause of the store clerk down the aisle. "I'm so afraid of hurting you—I'm afraid of getting hurt," she said. She touched his cheek softly as tears welled up in her beautiful, sexy hazel eyes.

"Mary, I need you to try and put the past behind you and believe in me. I love you so much, and you can trust me." He held her by her shoulders and slid his hands down her soft, smooth arms to hold her hands in his.

"I want to trust you, I really do, but it's so hard…"

"I realize that, but we have some time to work on it," he answered.

"Not much time," she said sadly, peering into his eyes.

"I know baby, but every minute we spend together will convince you more of my loving you, you'll see. Every kiss, every dance, every moment we're together. I won't leave without showing you that you have become the center of my life. I want you to feel safe with me. I want to go knowing that you'll be here waiting for me when I get back."

God, Mary, I've loved you from the first time you reamed me out about the broken table and the fire."

She laughed and cried, and laughed again. "I was pretty mean to you."

"You were very mean!" He pulled her closer to him and kissed her again. "Now how's about we get up off this floor and finish your marketing?" They stood together, and as he held her hand in his, she breathed in the fragrance of the roses he'd given her.

"My mother's gonna hang us both out to dry," she warned him.

"Ah, don't worry about her, I think she started liking me before she found out I was a sailor. With a little more work, I can win her over. I finally got to you, didn't I?" He smiled that wry, half-smile again and took charge of the shopping cart.

"What's next on your list?"

Chapter 5

The next morning at 7 a.m., Jimmy and Mary met at the 42nd Street beach access lot and walked hand in hand to the boardwalk. There were only a few others present along the sandy vista. As they reached a lamppost, he swung her around to face him, pressed her against the post with his body and kissed her. As his strong arms encircled her narrow waist, she reached with both hands and tousled his soft golden hair. As he leaned into her, he locked his fingers around her back and kissed her neck. She held onto his muscled shoulders and thrust her head backward, submitting to the waves of passion that swept over them. Earthly cares and reasoning were distant now, at last they were lovers. Together, they slid away from the lamppost and she arched her back further over the railing; his kisses caressing and exploring every inch of her elegant, long neck and becoming softer, almost whispers, as his hungry young lips caressed every freckle below on her slightly-exposed chest. Mary's right leg bent and steadied itself against the middle rail as she gasped and writhed under the power of his touch, holding tightly to his strong forearms as she leaned further, further backward.

THEY NEVER REALLY LEAVE

Seabirds crossed overhead, singing hushed arias to the lovers, and even the obnoxious gulls were quiet and seemed to appreciate the tenderness of the moment. An elderly couple walking their black Pomeranian passed by and the old man paused and sighed, perhaps mourning his by-gone youth. Instantly, his unsympathetic wife chastened him and dragged him forward with a yank on the sleeve of his faded blue cardigan sweater.

The constant beat of the surf against the shore echoed its approval, too, as a gentle, hushed lapping that approached and ebbed in cadence to their lovemaking. Shhh… Shhh… it seemed to be saying to the world. Be still. All of creation, quiet yourself.

In this rapturous moment, the lovers knew that any word spoken could only take away from the what they were sharing. For the young man, weeks of pining and agonizing for the love of his life was over. For the woman, years of loneliness, distrust, and solitude were being erased by peace and trust, thawing her icy heart. Words were unnecessary.

There was laughter, however, as the boy drew his lips away from hers to fondle her wavy hair, wooing her with those penetrating cobalt-blue eyes, smiling that wry, half-smile again. As she looked into Jimmy's eyes, Mary was sure that she could see a future together, filled with devotion, tender lovingkindness and stability. In his potent gaze she saw that which she'd given up all hope for; unconditional love and acceptance, integrity, and she saw a man who would love her completely for the rest of her life.

She smiled as she thought about how physically he was a man, but he had the uncomplicated, sincere soul of a boy. The man studied her beautiful, alluring hazel eyes, and he finally saw in them trust, tenderness, and her unbridled longing for him. The lovers spun away from the railing and continued down the boardwalk, arms around each other, laughing.

All of their senses seemed to be super-sensitive. The smell of the breeze mixing with the ocean brine, the sight of the vast blue expanse that lay before them, the warmth of the morning sun. Their sense of touch was heightened, as the couple brushed against each other and every stroke of a finger, every contact that their bodies made fascinated them. No one had ever touched and caressed Mary so tenderly, so sweetly. The boy could not remember a more beautiful woman. Their eyes were full to overflowing with the sight of each other.

And yet, somewhere in the recesses of Mary's mind, a deep sense of guilt began to rear its ugly head. Her demon past was taunting her once again. What right have you to be happy, you ungrateful little pig, when your mother is so miserable? Why are you wasting a whole morning, meandering along this walkway, when you should be home taking care of your poor decrepit mama? Who do you think you are, someone who's normal? These same voices spent years reinforcing the facts to her that any pleasure only brought unspeakable condemnation and guilt.

She faltered for a moment, almost stumbling on her way, dazed and confused. James caught her in his arms and held her.

"Mary, what's wrong?" She didn't answer, only shook her head, held her chest and took in a deep breath, defying the "voices" for one of the first times in her life. She nearly collapsed into his arms as the world around her spun wildly about before slowing.

"Mary?"

"I-I'm okay. I just felt a little light-headed for a moment. I'll be okay." She held onto him tightly. "Hold me, Jimmy. Please, just hold me." And he did just that, wrapping his arms securely about her, rocking her gently and kissing her forehead.

"I love you so much, Mary," he whispered as he tenderly stroked her hair and held her close.

"I know-I love you too. I guess I'm just not used to being so happy." He wiped the tears from her eyes.

"It's going to be all right, Mary. I'm going to take care of you." Although she trembled in his arms, she knew he was right. The concern and love in his eyes spoke to her heart that morning, and she made a vow to herself to always believe in him and never doubt him again. There was so much for each of them to learn about the other.

"We should be getting back," Mary said.

"Yeah, I know. When can I see you again?" Jimmy pulled her close to him.

"I don't know-tonight? When I get off work at 9:30?"

"Where?" He didn't give her a chance to answer, but held her tightly and kissed her again.

"Pick me up at my house about 9:45, just so I can tell mother that I'm going out." Knowing her mother, inebriated or not, would be bubbling over with questions about Mary's "going out," she planned an abrupt explanation and a quick getaway.

"Great," he said, "I want to talk to her again about us."

"No, Jimmy, not yet. Let's just enjoy a few days of peace and quiet before she blows her top, okay?" Suddenly, he discovered a facial expression of Mary's that he would become very familiar with and take delight in over the coming years. There was this way she'd cock her head a little to the right, furrow her brow and purse her lips with a serious look that made her argument irrefutable. He couldn't help himself and laughed and kissed her again.

"Whatever you say, doll. I sure do love you!"

"I sure do love you too Jimmy." The lovers did not hurry to retrace their steps back from where they'd come, but instead stalled to delay their return to their separate mundane lives. Any hindrance to their being together seemed so mundane now. They stopped to watch a flock of gray pelicans circling an area of the water, fishing for their breakfast, and laughed as the birds would each soar upward gracefully only to turn and fall down out of the sky into the water as they drew in a catch from the sea. They watched as a troupe of sandpipers scooted toward the tide as it receded, digging for their meals in the wet sand, then sprinted back to dry ground as the waves washed in again. The May sun had risen well above the horizon now, and with it arrived increasing numbers of other sojourners, young and old, to stroll the boardwalk and enjoy the beauty of the seaside.

Suddenly, amidst the growing throng of locals and tourists that passed by them, James pulled a small box out of his pocket and knelt down on one knee. "Marry me." The girl's face turned almost as scarlet as her hair and she gasped, clenching a hand to her chest as she tried to draw a breath.

"James! What are you doing?" He smiled that wry half-smile as he opened the tiny jewelry box to reveal a modest but shimmering diamond ring and presented it to her.

"Mary, I asked you to marry me. And I won't get up until you say 'Yes'."

"Oh, my god…" Mary Bauer, the ice queen, the argumentative, discourteous, hostile witch of the Chesapeake Crab House was swooning again, barely able to stand.

"Will you marry me?" The boy was not backing down. "I want to know that you'll be here waiting for me when my ship gets back, Mary. Be my wife." There was applause and cheers coming from the onlookers now, and shouts of "Do it!" and "Marry him!" as people passed. She was crying and shaking, and went down on her knees to kiss him.

"Yes! Yes, I'll marry you." She wrapped her arms around his neck and kissed him. "I love you!" Cheers rose from the crowd that had gathered around them and, grinning ear to ear, James Gallant slid the ring onto her finger.

"Mary, I love you with all my heart." His piercing blue eyes peered into hers. "I'm going to make you happy, I promise. You've already made me the happiest guy in the world—and I'm going to love you with everything within me forever." They kissed again, this time as ones fiancees with a whole lifetime of companionship and love ahead of them.

"Mary?"

"Yes?" she answered, trying to pull him up to stand.

"Would you marry me tonight?

"What?" she gave him a bewildered look. "Tonight? Really?"

He grabbed her brusquely and kissed her, pulling her tightly to him again.

"Yes—yes I will! I can't believe this is happening, but yes Jimmy, I will marry you tonight!"

He smiled that winsome smile again, and they were on their way. Tonight would be one of the most wonderful nights of their lives!

Chapter 6

Mary had a suitcase and a couple bags stowed in her car full of everything she would need for a few nights out of town. Chet told her to take as long as she wanted off from work. She left a brief note on the kitchen table for her mother who was out for the evening with Frankie. James picked her up in front of her house at 9:40 p.m.

Mary was wearing a simple white chiffon dress with a scoop neckline that was bordered by tiny, delicate yellow daisies. She put her bags in the backseat and James handed her a nosegay of white sweetheart roses, miniature carnations and white lace with pink satin ribbons. She kissed him and they drove twenty minutes to Norfolk where the Justice of the Peace was waiting to perform a quick ceremony.

By 10:15 p.m. they were pronounced husband and wife and were on the road to Richmond where the groom had made reservations at the prestigious Avamere Hotel. The ecstatic couple barely noticed the 76-mile drive north from Norfolk. At 11:45, they were checking in at the lobby of the hotel as "Mr. and Mrs. James Gallant."

Mary's eyes widened as the bellhop opened the door to their

honeymoon suite on the fourteenth floor. The room was elegantly furnished with a light oak four-poster bed covered with a large white goose-down comforter and elegant silk pillows. The floor was a soft white cloud of a shag rug that your feet sunk in as you stepped through. Long, lacy white curtains covered the large glass window through which a dazzling view of downtown Richmond could be seen. A modern-styled light oak dinette set was situated along one edge of the window. A 20" black and white television sat upon a matching oak stand and there was an elegant armoire and chest of drawers and a spacious closet. The bathroom was likewise decorated in gleaming white accents and brass fixtures. James nodded to himself, noting that the three vases of white roses he'd requested had been placed on the nightstand by the bed, another on a pedestal by the window, and another on the dining table. On the bed lay another dozen white roses, with a crimson ribbon that said "I love you Mary" in bright gold glitter. A bottle of champagne was chilling in a sterling silver ice bucket. Two champagne glasses on the oak stand beside the armoire.

"Will there be anything else, sir?" the bellhop asked.

"No, everything's perfect, thank you," James said, pressing a twenty dollar bill into the young man's hand.

"Thank you sir, and enjoy your stay at the Avamere." He closed the door as he left and the young newlyweds were alone in their massive, luxurious suite. Jim drew his bride close to him, they kissed and her wrap and handbag dropped to the floor.

"So, whaddya think?" He couldn't wait to ask, as they both stood there in awe.

"I think you're wonderful, Jimmy, and that you spent a whole month's salary on this place. I've never seen anything like it!"

"Nothing's too good for my wife," he beamed, and they sunk together into the downy softness of the bed, held each other, and kissed. There couldn't be two happier people anywhere on the earth tonight, James thought. They lay there together for quite some time, just kissing, touching, and holding each other, both of them content just to be together. He began to speak, but she held a finger to his lips, and lifted his chin to kiss him. She covered his face with kisses, kissing his eyelids, his nose, his eyebrows, his chin, his lips… She ran her fingers through his hair and her hand went down his neck to his sturdy shoulders and pulled him nearer. She loosened his tie and opened the top five buttons of his white dress shirt. She slid the black suspenders off his shoulders and lavished her kisses on his bare chest and stomach as he giggled and leaned over to kiss her again.

"I'll be right back," she said and grabbed her overnight bag and closed the bathroom door behind her. When she emerged seconds later…

"Oh-my-god," was all he could say. She was wearing a short black, satin and lace negligee, her scarlet hair falling across her silky shoulders. As she came to him, she pulled him to a standing position, unfastened the remaining buttons of his shirt and cuffs, slipped it off him to the floor, and pressed her hands across his chest and shoulders.

"Make love to me," she whispered.

"Oh, Mary, I love you. He picked her up in his arms and tenderly laid her on the soft bed, as though she was a china doll that he could crush, if not gentle enough. Long into the night, they made love repeatedly, exploring each other's body over and over.

How very different it was with the one you loved, she thought, making love to you Jimmy, she thought. Mary became a new woman that night as she became a wife, feeling sure that she would be no longer haunted by tortured visions of her past; a woman who finally had found the man she'd never dared dream existed. A man to share her life with, to love and trust completely, to be with every night; it occurred to her that she couldn't wait to spend the rest of her life with James. Somewhere in the early hours of the morning, when light from the breaking dawn outside their bedroom window cast a glowing luminescence on the lovers, with her head laid on his chest, she spoke.

"I don't want this night to ever end, she said," as her husband's eyes opened and met hers as he smiled that wry, half-smile and stroked her hair.

"I know, me neither," Jimmy said. She nuzzled against his chest.

"Tell me you'll always love me, James."

"With every breath I take, with each beat of my heart, as long as there's life in this body, I will love you forever and ever, my sweet Mary."

"I—I want to make you happy," she whispered with a touch of worry in her voice.

"Oh, babe-you do. You will. You're everything I ever dreamed of. I love you and I'm going to spend the rest of my life doing whatever I can to make you happy."

"I never knew it could be this way," she said softly. "I never knew anyone could want me like you do."

"I want you and I need you, Mary. I'll always need you, Mrs. Gallant." He held her close and they both drifted off to sleep.

****

I woke up this morning with the the most wonderful woman in the world beside me, my wife Mary. At first I blinked as my eyes opened to the unfamiliar surroundings; but now I lay here silently beside her, watching my beautiful bride sleep. Her face is radiant, I've never seen her look so peaceful. I don't want to move or touch her for fear of waking her from her rest, but it's almost impossible to keep my hands off of her! She's everything I ever hoped for, and she loves me. I want to give her a life she never dreamed of. I want to make her life happy, make her feel, at last, safe. She's so unique-so strong willed and yet so vulnerable. Thank you, God. Thank you for bringing Mary to me and helping her to see that she can believe in and trust me. Thank you for this happiness I'm feeling.

I love watching her sleep. I want to make love to her again right now, but I can't bring myself to awaken her, my gorgeous sleeping bride.

I can't wait to show her off to my family. Chief Collins was so good to give me a few day's leave on such short notice, with only barely a couple weeks left before the deployment. Mom is going to love her-everyone will love Mary. Propped up on one elbow staring down at her, I'm grinning like a fool.

The ship. Oh, man, I wish we weren't going out to sea right now. About three months in dry dock would be perfect. Long enough to find a place to live and get Mary settled in an apartment before I leave. But I don't have months, I have only weeks to find a home and get her settled in and make sure she doesn't feel deserted and helpless like her mom did. I have to make each day and every moment count toward proving my love to her. I've got to make her know for sure that the thing with Sandy was a big mistake—it only happened because I'd had too much to drink. "Like father, like son." Resonates through my head and I fight the temptation to ponder anymore of that.

She mumbles something in her sleep that I can't quite make out and turns closer to me, the white satin sheet sliding down to reveal her beautiful breasts. With one arm tucked under her head and the other on my stomach, she breathes in slow, steady breaths.

Oh, man! I want to make love to her again right now! As the room lightens with the rising of the sun, I wait for her to stir and open those sexy hazel eyes; and I'm hoping that she'll awake as ready as I am for more lovemaking. Oh, thank you God.

It seems as though she heard my thoughts and just opened her eyes, smiling at me and pulling me into her. We make love again and I know I've never been this happy before. Afterward, I hold my beautiful bride in my arms as she strokes my chest and hums some song I don't recognize. We linger there together for a long, long time before either of us wants to get up. Finally, I kiss her on the forehead and head for the bathroom. When I get back, I see the clock says that it's 7 a.m. Her eyes are closed again, so I go to the window and gaze down at the bustling streets of Richmond. I thought traffic was bad in Virginia Beach, it's nothing like this place. One of the larger highways I see is backed up for miles, with cars, trucks and buses-miles of headlights on one side and of taillights on the southbound highway. I'm so grateful to feel so far removed from that rat race for a few hours, up here with my darling bride.

"Hey, you. Get your cute bare butt back in this bed," she calls to me.

"I was just thinkin' about taking a little walk out there on the ledge," I tease.

"You what? Get over here, you're nuts."

"Yeah, baby, I'm nuts over you, but right now I feel like I could fly, so there wouldn't be any real danger out there." She sits up and fluffs the pillows under her, smiling and shaking her head.

"Well, maybe I'll clip those wings and you'll never be able to fly away from me." She patted the bed, "C'mon, honey, I missed you while you were gone."

"No you didn't, you were sleeping," I correct her.

"That's not true, I was just resting, waiting for my prince to come and make love to me again." I run over to the bed and jump on her and we wrestle for a few minutes until she calls "uncle."

"Mary, are you hungry? I am. Where's that room service menu?"

"Yeah, I'm hungry too-it's in the left-hand drawer honey." We order and then shower together quickly and don the complimentary bulky cotton robes just in time to answer the door. As we sit at the dining table, I take a sip of coffee.

"Mrs. Gallant, did anyone ever tell you that you are really gorgeous in the morning?"

She laughs, "no, but my mother has accused me of looking like 'death warmed over' on several occasions."

"No way, I think you're even more beautiful in the morning, maybe a certain way you look before life's demands and burdens start clouding your face again."

"That's sweet." She plays footsies with me under the table and I laugh. We both laughed a lot, that first morning as a married couple, exchanging more "you think your family is strange, listen to this..." stories.

After we finish breakfast, she says she wants to call her mother. I give her a look of concern. I say, "You sure you want to do that already, hon?"

"Yeah, I just want to make sure she's all right. What's the worst she can do-bitch me out over the phone?" She sits back on the bed and dials the number as I tug at the ties on her robe and she brushes me away, grinning. She sits up, bracing herself for a verbal confrontation with her mom. I lay down beside her and run my fingers through her hair. She waits as the phone continues to ring at her mother's house, then looks at me, puzzled.

THEY NEVER REALLY LEAVE

"That's weird, no answer."

"Well, maybe she stayed at her boyfriend's place."

"No, she never does that anymore. She says there's too much noise in his neighborhood, and no matter how loaded she gets, she has trouble falling asleep. Besides, she hates his apartment. It's overrun with cats- I mean, the guy must have eight or ten cats."

"You're kidding."

"No, really. He's always picking up strays alongside the road." She hung up and dialed again. Still no answer. "I guess I'll have to try again later," she says, a little worried.

"Hey babe, I'm sure she's fine. Like you said, we'll try her again in a little while. I know! Let's call my mom and tell her." She half-heartedly agrees and hands me the phone.

"Hello, mom? This is Jimmy. How are ya? Uh-huh." I smile at Mary. "Oh yeah, I'm doing great, Mom, just great. I've got a surprise for you though. You'll never guess what I did last night. Are you ready for this?" My mom cautiously tells me to go ahead.

"Well, mom, I got married last night! Yeah, mom, we're on our honeymoon in Richmond right now. Oh, mom, you're gonna love her." I reach over and hold Mary's hand. "Her name is Mary, mom. She's so beautiful, and we're crazy about each other. Yeah. Uh-huh. She's from Virginia Beach. Yup. That's right. We met at the restaurant where she works. Yeah, I know it's a big step. About three weeks or so. But mom, it's like we've always known each other. Here, I want you to say 'hello' to each other."

"Okay, honey," my mom says. I hand Mary the receiver and she looks terrified and pushes it back at me. I try to make her take it and we're playing hot potato with the telephone.

"No, Jimmy-not yet. I don't know what to say." Mary protests.

"Say 'hi', then. It's just my mom, trust me. C'mon honey, don't be afraid."

With her teeth clenched, Mary pleads. "Jimmy, no! I don't know what to—"

Back and forth the receiver is passed between us until Mary finally gives in which I knew she would, and speaks into the receiver. "Uh, hello, how are you Mrs. Gallant?" She playfully gives me a dirty look. "Uh-huh. Yes. Oh, thank you, that's nice of you to say. Yes, I can't wait to meet you, too." I hold my hand over the phone and whisper to Mary.

"Tell her I've got some days off so I'm bringing you home tomorrow." Mary's eyes widen with the news and look at me with shock, but then she repeats what I said.

"Oh. Oh, yes. That would be nice. Uh-huh. I can appreciate that. Yes, he's a wonderful man. Okay, here he is again." She thrusts the phone back into my hand.

"Mom, isn't she great? I can't wait for you to meet her. She's terrific. Yeah, we'll be heading out later today, should be there sometime tomorrow evening. Okay, mom. Yeah. I'll tell her. Okay. Bye. You too." I know that I must be beaming as I hang the phone back on its cradle.

"She said to tell you that you sound real nice," I tell Mary.

"Yeah, well what's the idea, shoving the phone at me like that? I was scared to death!" She playfully slaps my shoulder.

"I'm sorry, honey. I just wanted her to hear your voice. You'll love my mom, you really will," I said as Mary's face clouds over with worry.

"What's she going to think about the difference in our ages?" she asked.

"Oh, I hadn't thought about that. And you know what, I know she won't either—c'mon, you worry too much!" I kiss her and she looks a little relieved.

We're so rejuvenated after our breakfast, and I'm really jazzed after the phone call. We make love one more time in our honeymoon suite. Then we packed our things, check out at the desk, hop into my car and headed north on I-95.

Chapter 7

As soon as we drove up the onramp onto I-95 and headed north, I wished we could turn right around and head back to the honeymoon suite that had been our romantic sanctuary for the night. It's not that I didn't want to meet Jimmy's parents, but I've never been that good at meeting new people. Least of all, the whole bloomin' family of my new husband. Last night's magic and romance still had my head in the clouds-I'm Mrs. James Lee Gallant now.

I've never been more happy. I asked myself, "Why wouldn't Jimmy's parents like me?" I reached across to touch his shoulder lightly, and he glanced over at me and smiles that smile, melting my worries away.

"I love you, babe." he said as he brushed my cheek with the back of his hand. What if his parents do think I'm too old for him? I'm afraid of disappointing them and I don't even know them yet.

As we turned Northeast onto Route 17 to bypass the Washington beltway, the clean, freshly-painted white Virginia fences give a dignified order to the horse pastures that they guard. Oh crap. I forgot to try calling my mother before we left the hotel. Where was my head?

What if she fell and can't get to the phone? What if there was an accident? Oh get a grip, Mary-you know she's fine. She always is. As long as she has her scotch and cigarettes, there's nothing more she really needs. Even poor Frankie was small consolation to her, and she'll send him packing if something better ever comes along.

Suddenly I started mentally counting the service stations and back-road diners we're passing by, and I start fidgeting.

"What's wrong, babe?" Jimmy—it never takes him long to find me out. "C'mon honey, I can see something's bothering you. What's up?"

"Oh, I was just wishing that I'd remembered to try my Mom's house again before we left the hotel." He nodded and pulled into the next cheesy diner we came to.

"Let's go in for a cup of coffee and see if they have a payphone," he said. I've never known a man like him; no departure from his plans provokes him, he accedes to my every wish and doesn't give it another moment's thought. I sure love this man and I feel very lucky that he loves me.

"Baby, you're the greatest," I said, already relieved and feeling better. Mother will be hung over and mad as a wet hornet, but at least I'll know she's all right. Jimmy pulled the Monte Carlo up to the diner and parks. We hurried inside-the morning air still had a chill to it and we weren't dressed nearly warm enough for it. There's a small booth in the back and we passed a payphone on the way. He gave me some quarters and dimes and points to it.

"Go ahead, baby-I'll order our coffee." I dialed and the operator told me to put in $1.25 for the call. The phone began to ring on the other end, and I glanced back at Jimmy and smiled cautiously. I lean against the wall and hike the straps of my purse up my shoulder as two attention-starved, aging truckers began giving me the eye. I turned away from them and face the phone as I wait for her to answer. Still ringing. C'mon, mom. I can just hear her cussing the phone for interrupting her snooze. I looked back at James and shrugged just as she answers on the other end.

"Who th' hell are you and whattayou want?" Yep, it's her.

"Mom, it's Mary." I waited for the eruption, but she surprised me. After a long pause she said, "I got your note."

"Mom, I know you must think I'm nuts, but this is for real. He loves me and I'm crazy about him, too. You should have seen the room he got for our wedding night. It was all white with all these white roses and champagne—"

"You're wedding night? So you went off and done it. You really did? What do you want me to say, I'm glad for you?" She belched and apologized.

"Mother, I have a right to have a life—"

"Don't start that bull with me, girlie. 'Mother, I have a right to a life,'" she mimicked me. "You don't give a damn about me. You never listen to my advice and you think you know so much more than me." Tears began welling up in my eyes, as much in anger as in hurt, and Jimmy was instantly beside me, motioning for me to let him take the phone. I shook my head no, so he just put an arm around my waist and kissed me on the neck. "He really married you, I mean, with a ring and everything?"

"Yeah, mom, with a ring and everything. That's what I'm trying to tell you. We got married last night by a JP in Norfolk and went up to Richmond to this beautiful Altamere Hotel. Now we're headed north to see his family."

"Well ain't that just gonna be quaint."

"Will you stop?" Sometimes I really hated my mom.

"So tell me, are you in trouble?" She asked with sarcasm in her voice.

"Mother!" Even if she was drunk and hung over, she didn't have to be so mean.

"Well, are ya knocked up or not?"

"No mom, I'm not pregnant. And I don't appreciate that." I started to wonder why I was so set on calling her. There was a pause on the other end of the phone.

"When will the happy couple be comin' back down to this crap hole of a town?"

"I guess in a couple days, mom. Jimmy's ship is leaving in a week and a half. We have a lot to do before then."

"See? I told you about those damn sailors. Well, whatever. I got a freakin' headache you wouldn't believe, so I'm gonna go lay back down."

"Mom, I'm sorry it had to be this way. I would have told you if I thought you'd so much as try to understand. Are you really mad?"

"Like I said, I read your note. Of course I still love you, ya damned kid, you're my daughter, aren't ya? I just hope you know what you're doin'."

"I do, mom." I finally breathed.

"Well, I knew he was a ballsy one when he showed up here to talk to me about you."

"Yeah, we'll talk about your using the Louisville Slugger another time, mom, you really hurt him."

"Hurt him hell, he's lucky I didn't kill him."

"You're gonna really like him when you get to know him."

"Yeah, whatever, I gotta go lay down now."

"Mom-I love you." There was a short pause before she cleared her throat and spoke.

"Yeah, well, ditto. Bye." She plunked the receiver down.

Jimmy looked concerned, "How bad was it?"

"Bad enough, but not like I thought it was going to be." I took a deep breath and exhaled. I shook with laughter and relief as I wiped tears out of my eyes.

"Boy, I'm sure glad that's over!" He led me by the arm to the booth where our steaming coffee was waiting. It felt like the weight of the world had been lifted from my shoulders. She wasn't happy, but she was okay. Neither of us was hungry, so we sipped our coffee and laughed as we talked about my mom, then asked for our check. I couldn't help but reach out and touch that blessed, grimy payphone on our way out. I could have kissed it.

As we headed north again the lush greenness of the pines standing sentry along the highway waved their branches at us as we passed by. It seemed like a tropical rain forest compared to the hot, sand-whipping breezes and raggedy palms along the Virginia shore. With one crisis, the showdown with my mother over with, now my mind set itself to worrying about meeting Jimmy's family. What if they didn't like me? What if they thought I was too old for him, or not good enough?

"What is it now, baby?" It never takes him long to find me out.

"Oh, nothing, honey. I mean, I'm just glad everything is going so well. You know, with my mom and stuff." He smiled his cute, wry smile at me and winked.

"And you're worried that it won't keep going so well when you meet my parents."

"Well, yeah. I don't know. I just hope they like me." He reached over and caressed my cheek.

"Baby, there isn't anything about you that they won't love. You just watch and see. You don't need to be worrying, honey. Trust me." I was trying with all that was in me to trust him. I smiled, thinking how good it felt to have someone looking out for me, for once. I would have to learn to fight the doubts that tried to invade my peace of mind.

****

"Mary, baby. Mary… wake up, honey, you're dreaming."

I opened my eyes, sit up in my seat and stare back at him. Outside my car window, butterflies and bees are dancing about orange and yellow daylilies and someone's dog is barking.

"That was some dream you were having," he said.

"Uh, yeah, I guess so… where are we?"

"The last town we passed was Lucketts. We're still in Virginia, but we're almost to the border. About twenty miles from Frederick, Maryland. I had to make a pit stop-do you have to use the restroom, honey? Shoot," he laughed, "whatever you were dreaming about, you sure were mad!"

I didn't tell him—it was a nightmare about the sexual abuse that I went through years ago—I wonder when these dreams will ever stop. I got out of the car, stretched, trying to shake my mind out of the bad dream and headed for the ladies' room without a reply.

****

Within 10 minutes of being inside Jimmy's parents' house, I realized how foolish I was for agonizing over meeting Jimmy's parents.

"Oh, Jimmy, she's beautiful!" his mom exclaimed as she threw her arms around me and hugged me.

"I told you, Ma," Jimmy beamed with pride. I felt the blood rush to my face and tried to smile, although inside I was still really nervous.

"Congratulations, son," his dad said as they hugged. "Come on in here, you two must be tired from your trip." He motioned us inside and took our coats. Jimmy had been too modest when describing his parents' home. Compared to the aged, decrepit house on Fulton Street back home, it was a mansion. The sterile white foyer had a light gray marble floor and glass chandelier and it led into the formal dining room where we passed a long, elegant table and chairs and ornate china cabinet. I was a little overwhelmed as they whisked us through to the living room as though everyone lived this way.

In the living room, we each made ourselves comfortable on a plush, overstuffed love seat and sofa that were nestled before an open fireplace. A large pine log snapped as it burned and filled the room with as much warmth as Jimmy's parents did. His mom asked if we were hungry, and we both nodded.

"Is that cinnamon rolls I smell, Ma?" Jimmy smiled as she nodded and stood to go to the kitchen.

"Could I help you?" I asked.

"Why, thank you, dear, that would be very nice. The kitchen's right through here."

We emerged a few minutes later with fresh steaming coffee and a tray of freshly-baked cinnamon rolls. I noticed that Jimmy's eyes sparkled as he watched the two of us come in the room together.

"See, I told you they didn't bite!"

"Oh, Jimmy!" I slapped him lightly on the arm, embarrassed for them to know how much I'd worried about meeting them. The four of us talked for hours, no one taking notice of the time until it was 2 a.m. and someone looked at their watch.

"I'm so embarrassed to have kept you two up so late after your trip," his mother exclaimed. As we stood and said our good-nights I assured her that I had really enjoyed chatting with them, and all the stories about Jimmy when he was growing up. I laughed and said that I needed to tell them the story about how their son almost burned down the restaurant that I worked at, but Jimmy thrust his arm around my waist, leading me away.

"Oh no, you don't! That'll take another two hours to tell!" He laughed too. "That one's gonna have to wait until morning!" His mom said she had the guest room at the end of the hall freshened up and ready for us. "Alone at last!" Jimmy grinned as he pulled me in the room and closed the door behind us, pulling me close to him for a long, passionate kiss. "I love you baby. I love you so much."

"I love you too, hon. I'm so relieved that my first meeting your parents is over, I feel really silly to have worried so much. They're so nice and I can't say how comfortable they made me feel."

"I know," he answered. "That's just the way they are. Besides, who wouldn't love you? You're irr-resistable!"

"Shhhh, maybe they'll hear you!" I said pulling his hips toward mine. "This all seems like a dream, Jimmy. Like it's too good to possibly be true. Like any minute I'm going to wake up and find myself back at the crab house, exhausted and leaning against the kitchen counter waiting for my shift to end."

"It is a dream, baby. It's a dream come true." He held me tight, brushing my hair back across my shoulder. "And you have made me the happiest, luckiest man alive. Let's go to bed." He dimmed the lights and showed me where the bathroom was on the other side of the room.

I was still a little drunk with euphoria when I awoke the next morning with my head against my husband's chest, feeling his breaths rise and fall and hearing the steady beating of his heart. The morning sun poured through the sheer curtains between the mauve and ivory drapes and shone across my lover's golden hair. I fought the desire to reach up and tousle it, as I didn't want to wake him.

I smiled and nuzzled against his neck as I thought of my sweet, intrepid young husband, sauntering into his parents home with a bride seven years his senior, without any doubts or hesitation whatsoever. I could put up a pretty good front at the diner, acting like I was so calm and self-assured. But with him it went clear through. Beneath my hard exterior, I had been quivering and quaking with insecurity and fear.

I still have panicky moments when I can't believe this is real. Terrible, paralyzing moments when I just want to bolt and run before he awakens and sadly tells me that he's made a serious mistake, rushing into marriage. What would I do if something like what happened with Sandy occur again? I have to try to get beyond all these feelings of inadequacy and distrust. Jimmy loves me, and he's earned my trust.

"What are you thinking about, beautiful?" he said softly as he rubs his eyes and stretches under the weight of my head against his neck.

"Oh, nothing. Just about how happy I am." I hated lying to him, but he'd probably be really hurt to know how insecure I felt.

"I'm the lucky one, Mrs. Gallant," he grins. With one arm, he reaches around my waist to pull me on top of him and with the other, he brushes my hair back across my shoulders to cover my neck with his kisses. "I don't think I'm ever going to get used to being married to the most beautiful girl in the world." I kiss him to hide my embarrassment at his remark.

"I sure do love you, Jimmy," I whispered, touching his cheek.

"I sure do love you too, baby." Our lips are fitted together once more in a long kiss, and the thin strap of my negligee slips from my shoulder. He kissed my bared chest, caressing my skin, sliding the lacy neckline further down. We make love like two seventeen-year-olds, gasping and giggling and trying to be as quiet as possible in his parent's guest bedroom. As our passionate lovemaking reaches its climax, we both try to stifle our screams and fall back, spent and sweating on the bed.

As I try to catch my breath, I reach over to him and touch his chest. "Where did you learn to do that?"

"Do what, baby?" He asked

"Make love like that. I've never felt so wild-I could die right now and go to heaven!" He laughed at me and spanked me on the behind.

"I don't know-all I know is I've never wanted anyone as much as I want you baby."

We showered and dressed and went downstairs, where his mom was still in her robe and slippers, frying bacon and eggs. "Good mornin'!" she smiled broadly. "How's bacon and eggs and waffles sound?"

"Sounds perfect, ma," Jimmy said as he pulled out a chair for me and kissed her on the cheek.

"You weren't too cool in that room, were you? Your father had left the thermostat set to 72 and didn't remember it until we woke up this morning." Jimmy told her we were fine.

"Where's Dad?" Jimmy asked. Suddenly, her face clouded and she turned away, gazing out the window.

"Oh, you know your father. Ever since he retired, he seems to sleep later and later." She looked at him and they exchanged knowing looks, like a secret they were keeping. But Jimmy had already warned me about his father's drinking problem. It wasn't anything new to me, after living with my mom.

By Friday, we both regretted having to leave. It was the first time I could see worry on Jimmy's face; I could see Ralph's drinking worried both Betty and Jimmy. They both had learned as I had, that the less said about an alcoholic's antics the better off everyone was.

There were hugs and tears as we said goodbye and loaded the last of our things into the car. Jimmy's mom followed us to the car. "Here, honey, some cinnamon rolls for your trip."

"Oh jeez, Mom, thanks." Jimmy smiled. "You take care of yourself," glancing at his father in the doorway of the house waving.

"You take care of yourself, young man!"

"You know I'll be fine, Mom, I always am." Her voice caught in her throat as she gave her son one last hug. "I'll be praying real hard the whole time you're over there. Just remember, God's always with you wherever you go."

"I know, Ma." He kissed her cheek.

"And Mary, if you need anything, anything at all, please call. After you get settled, call us with your phone number and address, and I'll call you every weekend to see how you're doing. Maybe I'll even get Ralph to bring me down for a visit some day real soon."

That would be great-really. Anytime, I'd love to have you come down for a visit anytime." Jimmy opened the car door for me and his mom hugged me one more time before I got inside.

"You're a lovely girl, Mary, just what I've always prayed about for Jimmy. I'm just so glad that he found you." He kissed his mom's forehead and got in the car. As we pulled out of the driveway, I think we both had a knot in our stomachs and didn't talk until we'd been on the road for an hour.

"That was real tough," Jimmy said, breaking the silence as we drove south to Harrisburg.

"Oh, honey, I know it was." I patted him on the thigh. "Believe it or not, it was really hard for me, too. I really like your parents-both of them." He nodded slightly, his mind still back home with his mom and her alcoholic husband.

Chapter 8

"Well, hell's bells. If it ain't Duke and Dutchess of York, in the flesh." She mock curtsied.

"Good morning, mother. Are you going to let us in or not?" Mary was less than impressed with her mother's typical sarcasm, holding tightly to Jimmy's arm.

"Well sure I am! I just wish you'd a called ahead and I'd have had the police escort and red carpet treatment ready for you when you got here. Hee hee! And old Stanley down at the newspaper's gonna be awful disappointed he missed you too. Would've made the front page, I bet!" Jimmy just grinned at her as they pushed past her into the kitchen.

"Oh my gosh, mom, what's got into you? This place has never looked so tidy." It did look quite a bit better than the last time they'd been there, no dirty dishes in the sink, the floor had been swept and mopped, and a small vase of fresh flowers sat on the tiny kitchen table. Margie pushed her aside and grabbed the Jimmy's arm, leading him to a seat at the table.

"Whaddya mean, this is what my house always looks like. Don't you listen to nothin' she tells ya, kid. She always did stretch the truth a bit." Mary rolled her eyes and went to the counter to make coffee.

"You do have coffee, don't you mom?"

"Oh yeah, but I hope he don't take sugar-I've been outta that for a week. I forgot to pick some up yesterday when I went to the store." She pulled a chair up across from Jimmy, sizing him up.

"No m'am, just cream," he said.

Propped up on one elbow, she lit a cigarette and hacked violently for a moment. "Don't start that "m'am" crap with me, just call me Margie." She took a long drag on her cigarette and tried to straighten her tousled gray hair. "So tell me, Johnny, where'd you say your folks are from?"

"Mother, it's Jimmy-not Johnny. I told you—"

"Whatever. Was it New York?"

"Yes, Jamestown, New York."

She nodded her head, "over there where they got those skyscrapers and the Statue of Liberty and all…"

"Oh, no, m'am. I mean Margie. That's in New York City. Jamestown is a city clear on the other side of the state. Much smaller. She nodded and accepted a mug of coffee from Mary, averting her eyes to her daughter.

"So let me get this straight. You ain't knocked up, right?"

"Mother!"

"I'm just askin' an honest question." Mary's mother scrunched up her wrinkled face, eyeing both of their faces.

"I already told you on the phone, I'm not pregnant. Yet." Margie fondled the golden band and diamond ring on Mary's left hand.

"So it's for real?"

"Yes, Margie-it's for real. Fourteen-carat gold."

She shook her head in amazement. "A sailor with integrity. Never thought I'd live to see the day. You really love my girl Johnny?"

"Yes I do, very much."

"Mother, it's Jimmy. I told you before—"

Margie nodded. "You better, school-boy. This girl's been rooked and used by men every time she started dating them." She leaned across

THEY NEVER REALLY LEAVE

the table and stared him in the eye. "Cause if you do my girl like all the others did, I'll hunt you down myself until I find you." She leaned, hacked a cough and leaned back to light a cigarette. "I give you my word, kid. You'll regret the day you brought your sorry ass into this house."

"Mother, if you don't stop it, we'll walk out that door and won't come back. I'm not kidding. You better start treating Jimmy right." Her mom apologized and asked what their plan was now.

"We're going to find a small apartment either here in Virginia Beach or else on the base. Jimmy says the base housing isn't that great. Have you seen anything in the paper?" Margie pulled a newspaper from the top of the fridge with some ads circled in red and handed it to Mary.

"There's a couple, nothin' special. You know you always got a home here, girl, as long as he's gonna be away anyways."

Yeah I know, Mom-thanks. But I guess it'll put both our minds a little more at ease to have our own place. There's so much we need to buy to set up housekeeping, it'll probably take months and we'd run out of space here fast." Her mom said she supposed Mary was right, rubbed her forehead and took a long drag on her cigarette. Mary said it was real nice of her to offer, anyways.

"You're welcome. You'll stay here until you find a place won't you? I'll stay outta your hair, I promise." Mary looked up from the newspaper for her husband's approval and Jimmy nodded.

"We'll do that, thanks," Jimmy said.

The next five days sped by quickly, unfortunately. They looked at six different apartments before they found a kinda decent one-bedroom upper in Virginia Beach, just ten minutes from Margie's. It wasn't new, or even very nice, but the landlord said everything like the electric and the plumbing worked good. The day Jimmy paid $250.00 for one month's rent and security deposit, he picked up his very excited wife and drove to 1959 Trask Road to our new home.

"Well, babe-it sure ain't the Taj Mahal," he joked, as they hurried up the shoddy steps that led to the upper apartment in the rain. "Oh, this is great." The rain gutter had a huge hole in it just over the kitchen door and they laughed as he picked Mary up to carry her over the threshold and they both got drenched. Mary was undaunted.

Her eyes sparkled as she looked over the small apartment. "It's going to be perfect, honey!" She was really excited. Their first home. It appeared that the aged draperies had been cleaned and re-hung, and even the thread-bare brown shag rug in the living room looked like it had been shampooed. Fortunately, a stove and refrigerator were already in the kitchen. "Now, if we only had at least a sofa, a t.v. and a bed."

"We've got some shopping to do, babe. Place needs some furniture, huh?" They looked around at the empty rooms. Jimmy pulled the drapes apart in the living room and Mary cried out.

"Oh, just look at the view!" Mary wasn't one bit discouraged about the condition of the place. He'd forgotten the reason she'd liked the views of the ocean so much-the beach was within forty feet of the back of their apartment, and the grand Atlantic spread out before them in all its shimmering azure glory. "I love it-look babe!" Her eyes sparkled and danced as she pointed at the flock of pelicans flying over the water, barely skimming it, soaring in formation. She threw her arms around Jimmy's shoulders as they watched, and for a moment they didn't have a care in the world. We watched for a long time, then she turned to him with tears in her eyes.

"I know babe, I wish I wasn't going too. You know I wouldn't if I didn't have to."

"Oh, Jimmy. Why'd we have to get involved in that whole mess over there in Vietnam in the first place? Never mind, I know why. It just doesn't seem fair that you have to leave right now."

"Yeah, honey, I know. But we've got five days left before I have to report to the Forrestal. And I plan to make every minute of these few days count!" He held her by the waist and kissed her tender, pouty lips. "Whattya say we go get us a bed, for starters? The rain let up." She tried to smile and nodded okay. The closest place was on 32nd Street that sold furniture at a discount, only a few blocks away.

They picked out a bed, sofa, dresser and kitchen table at Weatherly's Hardware, and when the store manager heard about their dilemma, he pulled some strings and got their furniture delivered in two hours, just long enough for them to gather their things from Margie's and pick up a few groceries.

We should always live like we've only got five days left together, Jimmy thought. The scant furnishings, the daily unannounced visits from Margie and Frankie, not even the neighbors downstairs that argued incessantly could squelch their resolve to laugh, love, and make love for those five days. They laughed a lot and they cried a lot. They walked along the moonlit beach until midnight, then went home and made love until morning and slept in the next day.

Wednesday morning, Mary tapped Jimmy's arm as he still lay in bed. "Hey, husband. Get up. I want us to watch the sunrise together." He smiled and swung his legs around to sit on the edge of the bed, pulling her toward him and kissing her belly. Mary handed him a cup of coffee.

They sat together on a dune amongst the sea grass and beech elder and marveled at the dazzling sight unfolding before them. The sun rose up from the horizon as a fiery ball. As the sun climbs higher over the blue sea, the golden shadow over the water expands. It doesn't seem proper to attempt to describe the symphony of colors; glowing oranges, florid reds, shimmering canary yellows and brilliant hues of fluorescent red and soft lavender. The few clouds in the sky seem to vie against each other for positions to catch the brilliant colors. At low tide, even the wet sand assumes the cacophony of colors that the sun paints. Jimmy was sitting, his knees bent around Mary tightly as they sat in awe of the sight. He kissed her neck. They again watched the birds together, the pelicans flying south for the day, the little sandpipers scurrying in the wet sand as the waves brought in fresh food for them. The white caps were turning toward shore.

Jimmy awoke sometime during their last night together to find Mary propped up on one elbow, watching him and crying. He started to speak, but she pressed her fingers to his lips. "No-don't say anything. She just needed to memorize this picture of him laying there beside her. She needed to make sure she'd remember what he felt like, his smell, his soft touch, and his beautiful blue eyes. I'm so scared, Jimmy." She began sobbing.

"Baby... Scared of what, honey?" He wrapped his arms around her and pulled her close.

"Scared that you won't come back to me." She was sobbing harder and harder.

"Baby, why on earth would you think that? Don't you know I'm crazy about you? I'm your husband-we took a vow. You've gotta know how much I love you." He brushed the tears falling on her cheek with his hand, caressing her gorgeous red hair.

"I know, honey. I know you love me. But I just can't shake this feeling that you aren't coming back!" Her whole body was shaking and she buried her head in his chest and wept. "It's-it's just a horrible feeling that something is going to prevent you from coming back to me. Maybe it's all the years of mother's harping at me, or maybe it's got to do with all those men of hers, but it's so real! I just feel like I'm never going to see you again if I let you go!"

He rocked her in his arms and held her tight. "Ahh, honey. Nothing could ever keep me from you. You're all I care about-you're my whole life. I'm not going to let you down! How can I make you see?" She nestled her face into his neck and slowly calmed back down.

"Just hold me, Jimmy. Hold me like you'll never, ever let me go."

They stayed like that the whole remainder of the night. Neither could sleep, nor wanted to sleep. She couldn't shake the feelings of losing him, and Jimmy was wondering if it was the disaster with Sandy that was to blame.

"Honey, you know that I'll never be with another girl again, don't you?" He said.

She turned her face away without an answer. "Mary?" He tried to pull her back to him but she shot up out of the bed and turned around to face him.

"How can I know that for sure?" She asked. "How can I be completely convinced since that happened with that slut Sandy? There'll be liberty ports, and you'll be out with the guys, maybe drink too much and then..." She threw her hands up and clasped them behind her head. "What's to stop you from doing it again Jimmy?"

He sat up in bed and held out his left hand with the band of gold on it. "This," he replied. "Honey, when that happened I was really hurting. You had just told me that it was all over between us. I was confused, angry, hurt, whatever. And that girl took advantage of it. She only did it to hurt you, you know." He held out his arms to her but she made no move toward him. "Please, Mary. You've got to believe me. I don't want to live without you."

Mary just stood there as he spoke, arms crossed, rocking back and forth.

"Mare, remember our first date when I told you that I loved you? I have never said that to another girl. Never. It's true—pick up the phone and call my Mom if you don't believe me. I had only had a few dates in my whole life. And I haven't had any since I enlisted, besides you."

She finally sat down on the edge of the bed beside him. She knew that what he was saying was true. He had an expression on his face like a person whose world was about to end.

She nudged him with her shoulder and punched him in the arm lightly. "You better be sure, Mr. Gallant—or Mrs. Gallant will hijack a helicopter or somethin' and find you and kick your keister all the way back to Virginia!"

"Oh yeah?" He grinned and pulled her down on top of him. "Let's see some of that action here and now!" They wrestled for a moment and then began another session of love-making until they both fell back, spent, on the bed.

"Wow," Jimmy panted. I don't think I have to worry about the deployment—you're gonna kill me before I even get out of this bed!" At 5:15 a.m. they both drifted off to sleep.

Chapter 9

On July 29, 1967, off the coast of South Vietnam, God hid his face from the young crew of the USS Forrestal. While aircraft were being inspected and positioned for the second sordie of the day, a zuni rocket fell from a Mustang fighter jet and seconds later collided with a Skyhawk, spilling thousands of gallons of JP5 jet fuel across the flight deck. Everyone in the immediate vicinity was instantly covered with this liquid killer, and with one horrific whoosh! the jet fuel was ignited. Scores of young crew members and several pilots trapped in their aircraft were instantly engulfed in flames. Seconds later 1,000-lb bombs, some of which dated all the way back to 1942, began to ignite. As the first fell to the deck from the damaged aircraft, it detonated upon smacking against the 2-inch steel of the flight deck and exploded downward, opening up a crater through which the liquid hell, JP5 fuel, flowed and burned alive the crew below who were resting after a night of duty assignments. If evil has a face, it showed itself that fateful morning. In the carnage, the men of the Forrestal, many already wounded and bleeding, rapidly manned fire gear to battle the blaze that was engulfing the entire rear portion of the ship.

THEY NEVER REALLY LEAVE

Overhead aircraft coming to assist the Forrestal observed burning debris being blasted overboard by the force of the explosions, when the "debris" was in fact bodies. The entire ship shuddered with the force of the detonations. Whole fire crews battling the blaze were gone in an instant as the unsafe WWII bombs went off.

Many pilots lost their lives before being able to escape their aircraft. Young, new sailors and older, experienced sailors ran into the blazing hellfire and lost their lives trying to rescue their shipmates. These sailors were barely old enough to be called "men," who came from all over America. Detroit, Michigan. Portland, Oregon. And Macon, Georgia. They were buddies. They were brothers, fathers, husbands, sons, and at the very least, fellow shipmates. They were young men who had been properly trained and drilled over and over in firefighting and general quarters procedures, and when the time came to put their lives on the line, they did so without hesitation. The horror of that day in 1967 aboard the USS Forrestal will never be fully understood by anyone who was not present. And those who were present and lived to tell about it are reluctant to do so, understandably.

As the fires burned, men less experienced in firefighting found themselves manning the hoses of the lost fire crew members. Jimmy Gallant had been inspecting an aircraft aboard the ship and raced to join the others in the battle to get the pilots out of their aircraft and the burning and injured survivors to safety.

"Nelson. Nelson-is that you?" Jimmy couldn't believe his eyes. Rod Nelson lay on his side in the flames, injured by shrapnel from the explosions.

"Gallant? Jimmy?" he said weakly.

"Yup, it's me. I'm gonna get you outta here buddy. Don't worry."

"No way, I'm not gonna make it, Jimmy."

"Dammit, don't say that!" Jimmy shouted at his friend.

"You know I'm right," he moaned. Suddenly Jimmy saw the bloody, gaping hole in his shipmate's side, with a shard of steel embedded in it.

"You're gonna make it, Rod. Come on, I'm gettin' you out of here."

"Yeaaaah!" Nelson cried out as Jimmy tried to move him out of the flames. "Help the others, Gallant. Help someone who might live, not me." Tears and smoke smarted in Jimmy's eyes as he watched his buddy fading.

"Hang on, Nelson! Hey, over here! Help me get this guy to the tower!" Jimmy called out to another rescuer.

Rod Nelson summoned his last breath to say, "Jimmy, I said go on! I'm screwed and you know it! Just take my tags home for my mom and dad, okay? In case I get blasted to bits too, at least they'll know that I'm really gone. He whispered above the noise. "It might help them deal with it. And it'll mean a lot to me, too, Jimmy. Please."

"No damn way, Rod! I'm takin' you out of here!" Jimmy had taken off his blue aircrew jacket and was smothering the flames on Rod Nelson's clothing and flesh. "I'm not leaving without—you—Nelson. Nelson!" He shook his buddy, and burned flesh and blood stuck to his gloved hands. "Rod! Oh, God, no! Nelson!"

"Come on, kid, there's more live ones down there that need help. He's gone, you can't help him anymore." The officer pulled Jimmy to his feet. They started for the last few aircraft that still had pilots trapped in them, then Jimmy remembered Nelson's request and went back for his dog tags. He took off his flight deck helmet and slid the chain over his head, in such a rush he never felt the chain holding his own tags snap and fall to the deck beside his buddy.

"I'll get this one—you go for that last Phantom over there," the officer shouted. Jimmy nodded and ran through the inferno toward the aircraft. He was an electrician's mate, and he had no experience in getting a pilot out of an aircraft. The pilot was disoriented and in shock at what he saw going on around him. Jimmy climbed over the nose of the plane and motioned for the pilot to release the canopy and climb out. As the canopy lifted and the pilot unbuckled himself and struggled to break free from the tiny cockpit, Jimmy held out a hand to pull him to safety. But the JP5 had pooled enough under the plane that it ignited that aircraft's fuel lines. In an ear-splitting explosion, Jimmy was blown twenty yards away and laid there for several minutes before someone saw him move and realized he was still alive.

THEY NEVER REALLY LEAVE

"Hey, this guy's moving. Help me get him out of the fire. Quick!"

****

"Nelson. Petty Officer Nelson, can you hear me?" The military doctor shined a bright light into his patient's eyes, through the gauze wrappings that protected his face, trying to get a response. He motioned for a nearby corpsman to hand him the fellow's medical chart. "I can't believe he's made it this far. Nelson, if you can hear me, squeeze my hand. Nelson." No response. The man's vital signs were stable even though he was in critical condition from his burns and shrapnel wounds. "Poor young fellow—even if he makes it what kind of life will he have?" the physician thought. The doctor shook his head, made a notation on the chart and hung it back on the foot of the bed before he moved on to the next patient.

The main hanger bay aboard the Jefferson was nearly as chaotic as the firefight that was going on aboard the Forrestal. Helos rushed the injured and dying to the Jefferson flight deck, where they were guerneyed down to the hangar bay triage area on the aircraft elevators. The air was pungent with the smell of burnt flesh that hung from faces, appendages and torsos like over-melted cheese. The stench of fuel oil was everywhere, and with the comfortless, pitiful screams of the variously wounded men, some who had severed limbs. It was a hellish situation.

"Help me. Oh god, help me!" A young aviation boatswain's mate cries out as he realizes that he can't feel either of his legs, unaware that this is because they were both blown off by one of the explosions on the Forrestal.

Nearby, a Phantom F-14 pilot's charred body convulses involuntarily, his seared lungs desperately gasping for air as he dies. His is the lowest triage rating-#1, mortality imminent. A Navy Chaplain finds him and begins administering last rites.

The medical staff of the Jefferson was overwhelmed and unable to keep up with the constant arrival of casualties.

"Lieutenant, we just can't keep up-my god, they keep coming!"

"I know, Jones. There's more medical staff being brought in as soon as they can get them here. Just try to stay focused and keep calm as well as you can."

"Aye, sir," the medic was already exhausted, and it was only 5 hours since they started receiving the Forrestal's wounded. He raced to an electrician's mate who was trying to get up off his cot, despite his burns.

"Carter, Carter, where are you?" He cried out to a shipmate, but with no answer.

"Whoa," the corpsman guided him back down on his guerney. "Hold it right there, buddy, you're not goin' anywhere. That's right-lay back down, now. We'll find your buddy later. Right now we have to keep you still."

****

Mary was at work when she heard the news report about the accident. Reaching across to retrieve three plates of food for an order, she heard "We interrupt our programming to bring you a special news bulletin. The United States Navy has released information stating that last night, around 6 p.m. Eastern Standard Time, the USS Forrestal, off the coast of Vietnam, experienced a series of massive explosions and a devastating fire that engulfed a large area aboard the ship. While not releasing the cause of the fire, the Navy said there could be significant human casualties from the explosions and fires." Chet turned to see Mary drop the plates and collapse to the floor. "We repeat, the Navy has reported a series of massive explosions and fires aboard the USS Forrestal, with significant human casualties. The cause is yet to be determined, but it is not believed to have been caused by an enemy attack. We will bring you more information as it becomes available. We now return to our regular programming."

"Mary, Mary. Come on, kid-you okay?" Chet crouched down beside her on the floor. Chet looked up at a waiter who came into the kitchen. "Andy-get her a drink of water." The stunned waiter raced to the sink with a glass and handed it to Chet.

"What happened to her?"

"The radio. They just said there was an accident on the ship her husband's on."

He cradled her limp head in his lap. "Mary, come on babe. Don't just stand there, kid—go get one of the girls." Andy hurried out of the kitchen and returned with Sandy. Chet looked up, "You? Oh, well. Get over here, Mary's fainted."

Chet told her what happened. "Oh jeez, that's awful," Sandy feigned sympathy. "And they've only been married a couple months, too. Poor kid." She took Mary's head from him, putting a cool cloth to her forehead. "I'm sure she'll come around in a couple of minutes. You know, this same thing happened to me once. I was maybe eight years old-at my grandma's funeral. We went in the room and she was laying there all dead and stuff and I keeled right over. My mother said—"

"We get the idea," Chet growled and turned off the radio. Sandy looked wounded and tried to shake Mary awake. "Easy, girl. Don't give her a concussion," he said. Mary opened her eyes and the first thing she saw was Sandy leaning over her.

"What the—" She struggled to break free from Sandy's hold and sat up, bewildered by group that looked down at her. "What happened?" No one dared speak a word. "You again Sandy?"

"No, Mary. We ain't fightin'. Chet said the radio—" He motioned wildly for her to shut up, but Mary heard enough to remember.

"The radio? Oh—Oh my god. The announcement. The ship-Jimmy." She shook Sandy off and pushed herself to her feet. "Turn it back on."

Chet protested, "Mare, don't you think we should wait until you—"

"Turn it on, Chet!" She started toward it but he nodded and plugged the radio back in.

"...as we stated before, the USS Forrestal, home based here in Norfolk Naval Shipyard, has apparently been involved in some sort of accident with what the Navy is calling a 'significant loss of human life.' We will bring you up-to-the-minute updates as this story is unfolding."

"Jimmy," Mary whispered as she supported herself against the counter. Someone guided her into a chair as she stared at the radio. Chet sent everyone away and told Andy to take her home. She plodded up the steps in the rain and put her key in the lock as the phone began to ring inside her apartment. She picked up the phone, "Hello? Hi, Mom, did you hear the radio?"

"Yeah, I did. I'll be right over." Mary was standing in front of the living room window, gazing out over the stormy ocean as her mother let herself in the door. She felt like her life was suddenly as tempestuous as the rolling waves and dark sky. Was this the same house-the same life? Only a few months ago, she'd stood in this very spot with the only great love of her life, looking out over the azure horizon that reached miles out to the blue of the sky. Now, he was—no, she couldn't think that way. She just couldn't think that he could be—. Margie put some coffee on and walked over, putting her hand on her daughter's shoulder.

"Honey, I know what you're thinkin'. But you gotta try and be strong until you know if he was hurt. I bet he's just fine, and worried to death about you hearing about this. Every sailor on that ship is probably trying to get on a phone to call home." Mary turned to her mother and studied her face. Their relationship turned an important corner that day. In those few moments, the daughter who'd always had to be strong for both of them finally found a mother who could be strong for her. Mary couldn't remember a time when she'd cried on her mother's shoulder, but now she leaned over and awkwardly embraced the frail old woman and they wept together.

Later, as they sat together at the tiny kitchen table sipping coffee, Margie chain smoked and mentally made a list of her regrets. Was she ever close to her daughter? Maybe if she had been, Mary'd be happily married to some nice furniture salesman in Wilmington right now instead of going down the same road her mother had. Maybe she was too hard on her daughter all those times, maybe she drank too damned much. She knew she drank too damned much.

Was there something about her that wanted to see her daughter be hurt like she'd been? What a wretched woman she would be to jump on the chance to say "I told you so." She was feeling pretty ugly herself, and needed a drink badly. What was it all those years ago, anyway, that drove her man away from her? She looked across the table at her independent, strong-willed daughter and suddenly saw herself. As she stared at a spot on the wall, she could see herself walking along Surfside Beach with Thomas. They were laughing at the silly pelicans as they soared upward then turned and crashed down into the water, fishing for their breakfast. He was so tall, and so strong. She'd never been a strong person. And handsome, oh, he was so handsome. They had met at Kelsey's roller skating rink four months ago in April when his ship, the Roosevelt, came into port for overhaul. By August, he'd proposed to her and they began making plans to marry after his ship returned from a brief cruise. They made so may plans, from what kind of house they wanted to how many children. Children! She was going to be a wife—and a mother! Every day when he dropped her off at her mother's home she'd skip up the walk and fly to her room and wait for him to call her after he got back on base.

She could still see the men coming down the gangplank as they left the ship that December. She stood shivering among the entourage that greeted them. There were hundreds of people gathered there. One after another, she watched as a sailor was reunited with his family as Margie waited, bundled in her wool coat and scarf. The force of the crowd pushed her forward and back and she was so excited she thought she might burst. What had been a couple months seemed like years to her, and she had carefully X'd out each day on the calendar as she waited for this date to arrive.

She watched each eager girlfriend or wife greet her returning man. Where was he? She stood on tiptoes, leaning forward to pick him out of the crowd, looking left and right. As the crowd thinned out, the line of men coming down from the ship slowed and finally quit. Tommy? Why hadn't he left the ship yet? She found an officer and asked him about Thomas. He said maybe he was putting some last minute things in order but he would go back in and check. He suggested she have a seat on the bench while she waited.

When he returned forty-five minutes later, he looked puzzled. "Who were you looking for?" he asked her.

"Thomas Maine. Petty Officer Maine. You know, he works in, um, the boilers or the or something."

"M'am, I'm sorry, but I checked with the Personnelman aboard the ship. He never heard of a Petty Officer Thomas Maine, and he's the one who handles the records of everyone aboard this vessel."

"But that's impossible." She held fast to his arm. "This is his ship, the Roosevelt. You've just returned from your cruise. He told me to come here to meet him when he got back. You have to go back and check again!"

He shook himself free of her. "Lady, I told you. They never heard of him. This isn't his ship. Here's a number where you can check with the right department on the base that can tell you where he is. I'm sorry I couldn't help you more." She wanted to argue further, but fell back onto the bench and burst into tears.

****

Margie pleaded with the clerk on the other end of the phone. "Please, you have to help me. His name is Petty Officer Thomas Maine, and he's stationed on the Roosevelt. I guess he works on the engines or the boilers or something like that. I have to find him!"

"Ma'm, I told you, unless you're a family member I can't just give out information like that. Our military records are confidential. Maybe you should try to contact his family to try to find him. I'm afraid I can't help you."

She had waited all those months so excited to see him again, and as she stood dockside that day to greet him, she'd had a huge surprise to tell him that no one else knew. Now the huge surprise would be a dark secret. Without Thomas, she couldn't go on. Without his strength, she couldn't imagine her life anymore. Without Thomas, she couldn't bear to tell her mother that she was pregnant.

She took the next few days off of school to make more phone calls. She called the base again, she called the main Navy personnel office in Washington, D.C., she called the civilian authorities that they referred her to. Every military agency referred her to a civilian one, and every civilian organization told her to contact the Navy. They just weren't about to help a high school senior track down a man.

She couldn't tell her folks what she was doing, she couldn't tell them why she was placing all the calls. She hated having to go behind their backs, but in those days, girls like her were sent away. Her world was slipping away from her, and she couldn't see any hope without Tom. In a few months, she'd begin "showing", and then everyone would know. Her parents would be devastated and her life would be ruined forever—they'd surely make her give her baby away. She began to plan how she could run away from home and when to do it.

One Friday morning changed everything. Margie's mother Ada answered the telephone and it was the Bureau of Naval Personnel in Washington, D.C., stating that it was returning Margie's calls. After some more prodding, she found out that it was regarding a search for a certain sailor. When Margie got home that day, her mother sat her down and questioned her about the calls. Well into the third hour of the interrogation, Margie broke down and told her everything.

As she suspected, her parents were horrified and immediately set upon a plan to put her away and save the family name. After going through a long list of possibilities together, they finally decided to confide in her mother's sister Rosie. She lived alone just minutes away in Virginia Beach and had been in a few family scrapes herself over the years. She could be trusted to keep the truth under wraps. A phone call was placed and Rosie was happy to help them out. After they hung up, Margie packed a few things and they shuffled her off to Rosie's house.

As time would tell, she had almost given her baby up once before Rosie talked her out of it. That was a decision that she never regretted, except that she would like to have been able to give her little girl more. Rosie had been her Rock of Gibraltar. She wished Rosie were alive and here now, to help comfort poor Mary.

Margie made another decision that day that would require all of her strength and determination to stick with it. She was going to become the mother that Mary'd never had. If Mary would let her, she was gonna start being there for her every step of the way. And she decided that whatever it took, she was going to quit drinking.

****

"Hello?" The voice was distraught and shaky.

"Hi Betty, it's Mary."

"Oh, Mary. You dear, sweet girl. Thank you for calling us—I was just going to call you. Have you heard anything yet?" Mary fought back tears.

There was a hush on the line for a moment, then Mary spoke again. "I just found out about it at work. They had to send me home for the day. After I hear that Jimmy's okay, I'll be fine. Right now—I'm just going nuts."

Betty bit her lower lip as she leaned against the kitchen wall. She tried to find words to comfort her new daughter-in-law. "I meant to call you, but..." She smoothed her housedress and sat down at the kitchen table. "We've been listening to it since they first reported about it. I-I'm so worried too, I feel like tearing my hair out!" She broke down in tears, sobbing and Ralph took the phone from her. "What can we do to help, dear?" he asked. "If you need us to be down there with you, we'll be on the first plane out of here. I promise."

"That is so thoughtful of you, Ralph. Actually, my Mom insists on coming here to stay with me. I appreciate your offer though."

"Oh, of course. How sweet of your mom. She must be really special to have brought up a nice young woman like you."

Yeah, she's special all right, Mary thought. "Let's plan on calling each other at least twice a week or sooner if one or the other of us hears something, okay?"

Another pause and an awkward, silent moment. Only a few weeks before Mary had met Jimmy's parents and felt so at ease with them. Things had changed now. She was numb with emotion and words didn't come easily for either person. Betty had composed herself so Ralph handed the phone back to his wife.

"Okay, dear," Betty said. Just remember that our offer stands. We'll be there as quickly as possible if it would help you. You and Jimmy are both in our prayers." They exchanged good-byes; Mary hung the phone up and turned on the t.v. again.

Chapter 10

The television news anchor droned, "As we have reported to you earlier, some type of catastrophic explosion aboard the USS Forrestal which has been stationed off the coast of Vietnam has been reported by the military. Government sources say the explosion, or explosions, set off huge fires aboard the ship with an undetermined loss of life and damage to the vessel. Several other ships in the Forrestal's battle group have been transporting the wounded and dying to their own medical facilities to help care for them. We take you now to our Pentagon correspondent, Jack August. Jack, what do you have for us?" A young red-haired man in a trench coat gripping a microphone in the cold rain appeared in front of the Pentagon building.

"Well, Burt, Pentagon sources tell us that although the main fire has been extinguished, small fires continue to be found as a compartment-by-compartment search is being made. The crew of the Forrestal and fire crews from their battle group vessels are working around the clock to get the situation under control. While not ruling out the possibility of an enemy attack, we've been told that it appears more likely that a mechanical failure aboard a plane or planes that were loaded with ordinance for a morning bombing raid over South Vietnam was the cause."

"Jack, we're hearing that the medical department of the Forrestal has been overwhelmed with the injured, and that many are being transported to other ships for treatment. Can you confirm this?"

"That's right, Burt. The Navy hasn't released exact numbers yet of the dead and wounded, but they are using very specific language to prepare us to hear of significant losses. The battleship Jefferson has been probably the biggest help, with their medical crew evacuating and caring for the sailors from the Forrestal. Our sources here tell us it could be a day or two before a complete roll call can be taken to estimate the dead, injured and missing."

"Jack August, reporting live from the Pentagon." Mary flicked off the television and sunk back in the armchair.

"I don't know if I can take this, mom, this not knowing. I feel like I'm going crazy-how long can it take to find out he's okay?" Margie leaned toward her daughter from the couch, patting her leg.

"Now honey, don't talk that way. You're one of the strongest people I know, and I'm not leaving you alone for a minute. We're in this together, kid." She took a drag on a cigarette and coughed. "I've been thinking a lot ever since this happened, and one thing I know is that you deserve more'n what I've ever done for you. I love you, Mary, I've always loved you. But damn it, I realize I've let you down lots of times—all your life—now I'm gonna start trying harder to be the mother that you need." Her voice was shaky and she was self-conscious of the facial tic, tried to control it and looked away toward the window. "I guess one good thing that come of your growin' up the way you did was that it made you tough. You're gonna come through this one way or the other. I ain't sayin' I know for sure that he's okay, but if there's a God up there, he'll make sure your husband comes home to you. No one ever deserved a miracle more than you."

Mary marveled at her mother's words. She'd never seen her mother act so intimate and warm. "Damn you, Mother," she thought. Where was all this support all my life when I needed it? Why after all these years, did her mother suddenly wake up and seem to connect with her?

It made her feel weird. Happy, but weird. Even at holidays and funerals her mom had never showed a whole lot of emotion, she just wasn't that kind of person. You know she cared about what happened to you, but she didn't tell you. But as they sat there that Saturday morning there were tears in Margie's eyes and a wall inside her daughter's heart began to crumble.

****

Morning melded into afternoon, and afternoon into evening as the women waited together, somber but vigilant. The remnant of a tropical storm was skirting the Virginia coast, turning the Atlantic into an angry, pounding, tumultuous beast that punished the shoreline and sent most level-headed seafarers to shore. The bleak, gray sky painted an apt portrait of how Mary's heart felt as she tried to pray.

Dear God, I know I've never been a praying person like I should've been, but I don't know where else to turn. You know how much I love Jimmy. I guess you even know about this little baby I'm carryin'. Don't make this child grow up without a father like I did. Please let Jimmy be safe. Please! I'll do anything you ask from here on out—if you'll just bring him home to me. I promise, God, I'll try to be a better person, and read my bible more, and even go to church. Just bring him home, God. I can't go back to the way my life was before I knew him. I'm so afraid! Amen.

Mary opened her eyes when she heard her mother stir and light up a cigarette. "I know, honey, I've been prayin' too. Can't remember when I've done so much apologizing and praying to the Lord, matter of fact. Jeeze, it's after midnight already." Margie stood and walked to the window, looking out over the dreary view. "I'll be glad when this damned, uh, darned storm passes. Even the weather's depressin'." She took a drag on her cigarette and pulled her worn cardigan around her frail little frame, shivering. "Maria. Hurricane Maria, that was the name of the storm that was brewin' out there the day you were born. I almost named you for it, but settled for Mary instead, after your great-gram."

Mary smiled. "So I came in on a storm, huh?"

"You sure did, in more ways than one, honey, if you know what I mean. I remember laying in that hospital room with Rosie, waiting for you to come. She got me through it, sitting there with me the whole time. Lord knows nobody else in the family was there. The wind was howling around those old hospital windows and I could see the stormy sea outside. They almost had to evacuate us, you know." She crushed out her cigarette in the ashtray and laughed softly. "Yeah, Rosie—she just kept telling me that it would be over soon, and that it would be the worst pain I'd ever feel but the easiest pain to forget. She was right about it, too. As soon as I saw your beautiful shining little face, it was like God just came and dropped you into my arms." She sat down on the couch and rubbed her hands. "I just wished that—" she sucked air when she realized what she was going to say. "Oh, honey, I'm sorry."

"I know, Mom. I know." Mary leaned forward, studying her mother's face. "Uh, Mom, I think I'm pregnant." Margie was smiling and nodding.

"I thought so. You know you can tell when a woman's gonna have a baby."

Mary's hands went to her abdomen, softly caressing it. "We didn't have to get married, Mom. This happened after."

"Oh, I know, Mary. I was just giving you shi—I mean crap, back then. I'm gonna be a grandma! I can't believe it. And Jimmy's gonna be just fine—you'll see honey." Her daughter mutely nodded and stood to turn the television back on. Walter Cronkite was updating the report on the accident on the Forrestal.

"Word from the Navy tonight about the accident aboard the Navy aircraft carrier Forrestal tells us that as many as one hundred men have been lost in the carnage. As we reported earlier, an explosion of unknown origin set off a chain reaction of fuel-fed fires and other explosions of ordinance on the flight deck of the Navy vessel as it prepared for flight ops off the coast of Vietnam. A number of nearby ships have been assisting the Forrestal in battling the fires, which not only involved the main flight deck, but also part of the ship's hangar bay and several compartments below. Details are still very sketchy as we try to sort through various radio transmissions that have been received. A Navy spokesman has told us that names of the wounded and dead will not be released until their families have been notified. For now, we are told that beside the tragic loss of life and grievous injuries, the ship has sustained major damage and may have to return to port in Norfolk, Virginia, despite the fact that it has been on the front lines only a short time. We will interrupt any normal broadcasting when we have major new information to report to you. For now, this is Walter Cronkite, CBS News in New York."

"Oh my God, mom, a hundred men dead and who knows how many more injured? How can it be possible? You know Jimmy works on the flight deck. He's dead, mom, I just know it. Oh my God, it's your life happening all over again!"

"Hold on, Mary—"

"Shut up! Shut the hell up! I don't want to hear any more of your feeble attempts at consoling me. You've never been there for me, why should I think you'd be there for me now? You don't understand anything—We were in love! And now it's all over. What makes you think that after all these years you can just jump in now and become a mother to me? You're nothing but a drunk—A stinkin', stupid drunk!" She grabbed her coat and pocketbook and headed for the door.

"Where're you going, girl?" Margie called after her.

"None of your damned business." She bolted through the kitchen and slammed the door behind her. Her tires spun on the wet pavement as she sped down the street and turned onto Ocean Drive.

Speeding down the 15 mph zone at 55, Mary soared through intersections and lost control several times as she crossed flooded areas of the boulevard, sending sheets of water over the sidewalks. But the fury of the storm along the coastline was nothing compared to the furor going on inside Mary's soul.

Mary sobbed and screamed out loud. "Why God? Why did you bring another man into my life and get me to trust him and even fall in love with him?" The tears stung in her eyes. "How could you do that to me again? Some God you are—you couldn't care less about me and my life. My life's always been screwed up. And what do you care? Why do people believe that you care? I had one chance, one chance to finally find someone, and now you've taken that away from me!" She was pounding the steering wheel and veering onto the interstate. "You're cruel—that's what you are! She headed north as sheets of water pounded her windshield.

"I'll never believe you again, God. I'll never, ever trust you or any other man again. Mary didn't have a clue as to where she was driving. She only knew that she needed to be going somewhere else right now. With Jimmy, her life had had purpose. Now her life was as aimless as her destination on the highway. Nothing mattered anymore. It was humiliating and agonizing to realize that she'd been stupid enough to fall for it again. It just goes to show you. No matter how long you live, there'll always be another sweet-talking, promise-making man out there to break your heart. God! She hated herself for trusting Jimmy, for trusting God.

Jimmy. Why didn't he try to get out of the cruise to Vietnam? Could he have? Would he, if he could have? Damn you, Jimmy! How can you just die and leave me, and expect me to go back to the kind of crummy life I had before I loved you? I believed in you! I finally let my guard down with another man, another sailor, and this is what I get. You and all men can go to hell, for all that I care. Never, never, never again!

It was 2 a.m. on the car clock when she was sobbing so hard that she had to pull off onto the berm to park for a moment. With the motor running and the headlights blazing through the torrential downpour, Mary got out of the car and began running. After she'd passed out of the light her headlights, she kept running in the blackest night of her life. A heel broke on her left shoe and she kicked them off and ran on. Once or twice she had to stop to catch her breath, but then she'd race off again, down the berm of the freeway. A few motorists pulled over when they saw her to offer her help, but she waved each one on. Soon an 18-wheeler pulled off onto the berm and set its brakes. The driver got out and waited for the running woman to pass by.

"Hey, baby, what'cha doing out here alone on a night like this?"

"Just leave me alone," she said as she jogged past him.

"It's all right, baby. I'm just offering you a ride if you need it." He began jogging a few lengths behind her. His voice was low and raspy, menacing and guttural.

"I don't need a ride, just leave me alone." She glanced back nervously. He was following her.

"Hey, I've got hot coffee in my rig. Now doesn't that sound better than running out here in this downpour?"

"I said 'No,' now will you please leave me the hell alone?" But he grabbed her by the arm and stopped her in her tracks, and she could see a chilling smile on his face in the beam of the rig's headlamps.

"I can't just leave a pretty thing like you out here all alone in this storm. C'mon back with me and just get warmed up and then you can tell me your story, okay?" She struggled to break free from his grip.

"You go to hell, buster!"

"Come on, girl. Enough of this shit, I've been on this damned road forever and I ain't had sex for weeks. You be nice to me and I'll be real nice to you." He was dragging her back to his rig as she was kicking and screaming. There was not another vehicle in sight to witness the struggle.

"You bastard! Let me go!" She pounded on him and scratched at his face but it was no use, he overpowered her.

Back in the rig, he turned off the headlights and left the engine running. He forced Mary into the cab and she spit in his face and he slapped her. "Bitch! Just relax and enjoy yourself. I ain't never had a woman complain yet."

"Listen, mister, you can't do this to me. I'm pregnant, you hear? I'm gonna have a baby. You can't—"

"Yeah, right bitch. I don't want no more talkin' now. Just shut up." Mary struggled against him again and he slapped her. He pummeled her face with his fist, breaking her jaw, nose and several facial bones. She would never be the same again.

"No—!" Her last word as he bore down on her windpipe, cutting off her air and asphyxiating her into unconsciousness.

****

"Oh my God, Ethel, look at that over there," the man said to his wife as he pointed to the object in the culvert along the highway. He slowed the camper down and his wife squinted to see in the morning sun.

"George-it looks like a body! A naked body! We'd better get to a phone and call the police right away." They sped down the road as Mary's nude body lay in the ditch, beaten beyond recognition and stabbed several times.

****

You ask me how I'm doing? How would any mother be doing, sitting in a hospital beside her half-dead daughter who was found naked and stabbed in a ditch? After all, even a mother like me—a stinkin' drunk as I am, has feelings. With all my faults and failures, my Mary has always been the one good thing that came of my life. I gave life to her didn't I?—I loved her, even if I wasn't a model mother. I loved her dammit.

This stupid lady cop that's been hovering about the room waiting for Mary to wake up is startin' to really bug me. Probably all she cares about is getting the information so she can get back to her desk and file the report.

It's the doctor that I want to talk to. Wonder where the hell he is. I haven't been in a hospital room since Rosie passed on, I forgot how crummy they are. All the commotion, and the stench, all the pushy nurses. Laundry going down the halls on clattering carts. I hate hospitals, did I tell you that yet?

Mary, baby, hold on. You have to make it honey. Not only for me and Jimmy, but for that little baby inside you. Oh God! Don't let her die. I need a drink so bad. Did I promise Mary I wasn't going to drink anymore or just tell her that I was thinking about stopping? Did I say anything about it at all to her? I can't remember. Well, they can try to throw my ass outta here if they want to, but... Where's that little flask of Jack Daniels I keep in this pocketbook? Okay, there you are. Good-lady cop has gone for a toilet break. I can take a swig in peace. Bottoms up—oh yeah, that's better. One more. Yup, that's just what I needed.

"Are you family?" Margie about jumped out of her skin at the voice behind her.

"Damn right I'm family, I'm her mother. You the doctor?"

"Yes, Mrs.—"

"Just call me Margie." The handsome young doctor walked around the chair Margie sat in and lifted the sheet covering Mary, checking some bandages and a drain that was attached to her chest and abdomen.

"Margie, I'm Doctor Boyer. I operated on Mary after she came in. She was in very bad shape, still is; do you have any idea how she got out there on the highway like that?" The woman wiped her mouth and shook her head.

"We were at her home watching the news. Her husband is on that ship that had the explosions, the Forrestal. She kinda freaked out and started yelling at me and took off in her car, wouldn't even tell me where she was going. How bad is she, Doc? These dumbass nurses won't tell me shit. Pardon my french."

He walked over to Margie and softly placed his hand on her shoulder. "She's stable now, but she lost a lot of blood and may have a few broken bones. We had to get the bleeding stopped and check her internal organs for damage first. We'll have to leave the breathing tube in her for a few days—maybe a week. It all depends on how she comes along. It seems that she was beat up and stabbed repeatedly, Margie."

"What?" Margie's head swooned. "I can't—what kind of sonofabitch would do something like that to my Mary?" She clutched her chest. "You say she was stabbed?"

"I'm afraid so. She was found a half mile from her car, you know. Like she had car trouble or something and started walking. Someone must have picked her up, but from the bruises on her wrists we think she was forced to go with him."

Margie gritted her teeth, "That bastard must have been a brute—my daughter's a strong girl." The lady cop came back to the room and started taking down some notes from the doctor and Margie's conversation. "By the way, Doctor Boyer, have you met our 'Lady Sherlock Holmes' here? She's waiting to drill Mary for info once she wakes up."

The detective frowned at Margie. "Very funny, Mrs. Bauer. It's Officer Ross, doctor. When can the victim answer some questions?"

The doctor ignored the cop and leaned closer to Margie. "She was, uh, sexually assaulted as well."

"What the hell?" Margie stood, toppling the chair she'd been sitting in. "No! Doctor, she's pregnant! What about the baby?" Just then, Mary's eyes opened at hearing the word, and her eyes focused as she saw the downcast look on the doctor's face as he shook his head. Margie slumped across the side of the bed, burying her face in Mary's shoulder as her tears flowed longer and harder than they had in many, many years.

Mary was not discharged from the hospital until two weeks later, and during that time she refused to talk about Jimmy, the rape, or the baby. She stubbornly turned away food and resented Margie's daily visits. The only person she seemed to respond to favorably was young Doctor Boyer. He was gentle, and soft spoken, like Jimmy. He was never intrusive or demanding, and staunchly defended her silence to the police department. He wasn't about to let them harass a patient of his, they'd just have to wait until Mary was ready to talk about the attack.

While Mary seemed to be struggling each day to find a reason to want to live, her mother waxed stronger and even seemed to thrive more during the crisis. She appeared each day dressed smartly with fresh makeup and her hair done. Although she was an unwanted visitor in her daughter's room, and they seldom spoke more than a few words a day, she arrived mid-morning and lingered until the end of visiting hours.

On Saturday, Dr. Boyer came in Mary's room on rounds in the morning and told her that it was time for her to leave the hospital. He could see the apprehension in her eyes as he explained the medications she should continue taking and when she should see her family doctor again. He handed her a note with his office and home phone numbers, just in case she needed someone to talk to; obviously not a conventional discharge procedure. But he'd come to admire the strength, the tenacity to live he saw in Mary and had felt a special something for her in the few days that he'd known her. And it didn't hurt that she was one of the most beautiful women he'd ever seen. Patting her hand, he tried to reassure her that in time she would feel much better about everything. She just needed time and understanding, and he gave her a pamphlet about a support group for victims of rape that met once a month in the YWCA near her home.

"I feel like he's out there. Waiting for me. Like he knows I'm alive and he wants to finish what he started," Mary confessed. "The article about the attack in the newspaper might have warned him that I'm still alive."

He put his hands in the pockets of his white doctor's coat and reassured her. "He's probably halfway across the country by now. Maybe not even from around here, Mary. Your fears are not unusual, and that's why I recommend you attend this group, maybe even see a therapist. You've been through a brutal, senseless attack. But from what I've heard from the authorities, these maniacs seldom come back. You just need to concentrate on healing. Body, soul and spirit." He turned to smile at her as he headed for the door. "Good luck, Mary." Mary felt a tug at her heart that she'd never see him again.

Margie waited in the car outside the Emergency Room entrance as the nurse brought Mary down in a wheelchair. It was a warm, sunny day—so different from the day that she'd arrived in the hospital, clinging to life. The scent of roses and petunia beds would be what Mary would remember from that day, after the antiseptic smell of hospital cleaners and ointments and bandages for four days.

"Hi, kid. It's gonna be good to have you back home," Margie said brightly as the nurse helped Mary into her seat and closed the car door. Mary smiled slightly for the first time and nervously eyed the parking lot, a habit she would be a long time in breaking after the attack.

On Sunday morning, Mary slept late and awoke to the sound of Oral Roberts on her mother's television in the living room. Oral Roberts? she thought. Nah, she must be mistaken. She sat up on the edge of her bed to listen again. Yup, it was him. Her mother was listening to a religious service! She smiled, shaking her head as she slid into her slippers and robe, because the world was just changing too fast for her to keep up with it.

Margie ground out a cigarette in the ashtray as Mary emerged from her room. "You can wipe that smirk off your face, missy. I know what you're thinking."

"I didn't say anything, Mother." She yawned and stretched, barely keeping a straight face.

"Yeah, well I can just imagine what you'd like to be sayin'," her mother grinned as she stood and turned the t.v. off. "Whattya want for breakfast?"

The two women spent the day playing rummy and trying not to watch news broadcasts. They both knew that any day they would get the news—good or bad. If Jimmy was okay, he'd find a way to let them know.

On Monday morning, a bird was singing outside Mary's bedroom window. She couldn't tell what kind it was, but it was the most sweet-sounding, melodious song she'd ever heard. She lay on her bed just listening for the longest time. Having awakened to the serenade, she was disappointed when she heard the flutter of wings as it flew away and the song ended. Her thoughts turned back toward the memories of the attack that she couldn't censor from her memory. They rolled over and over in her mind and never warned her before setting in. What did she do to deserve it? Could she have fought harder? Prayed harder? She bounded out of bed to escape the thoughts, dressed and stood in front of her mirror as she brushed her hair. Where are you, Jimmy? Why haven't you called us by now? Why haven't we heard anything from the Navy either? For someone who usually kept her life pretty much under control, it was only chaos now. She was so afraid that she was going to lose Jimmy. She felt guilty for being angry at him for leaving. And there was a whole new whirlwind of emotion that the handsome Doctor Boyer had stirred up in her heart—as much as she didn't want to admit it. He had been her lifeline for those first several days after the attack. Although she felt in her heart that it was wrong to do so, she kept his phone numbers even after she'd decided that she couldn't ever call him. He was so strong, and so compassionate, though. Her whole life was turned upside down. She felt ugly and nasty for the way she'd treated her mom. What she saw in her reflection wasn't the same as the happy bride from a few months before. This woman was weak and scared, and she hated feeling weak—This woman was angry and violated and shamed, and so afraid to find out what had happened to Jimmy. So afraid not to find out. She looked like she'd aged 20 years in the last week.

Her scathing self-analysis was interrupted by a knock on her bedroom door. "Mary, you up?"

"Yeah, mom."

"Come on out here, honey. There's someone here to see you."

Chapter 11

The Navy officer sat erect in his clean white uniform in Margie's chair, holding his hat on his lap. He stood as Mary entered the room, motioning for her to sit down. With her mother by her side, he handed her a white envelope with the Navy insignia and her name on it.

He spoke, "Mrs. Gallant, the United States Navy deeply regrets to inform you that, during a catastrophic explosion aboard the USS Forrestal last week, your husband Petty Officer James Gallant was killed. The President and the Secretary of the Navy wish to convey their deepest sympathies and to express their gratitude for your husband's service to his country." Mary looked at her mother and forced back her tears. She leaned forward, elbows on her thighs.

"Jimmy? Please, there must be some mistake." She had the face of a victim begging her killer for her life. "He's careful. He said he'd be careful. We've only been married—oh, my God, no!" She collapsed into her mother's embrace and sobbed. The sad officer waited a few moments before nodding to Margie and leaving.

"Mom, no! He can't be dead. I don't even want to go on living without him. He's the only man who ever really loved me, the only man

THEY NEVER REALLY LEAVE

I ever really trusted," she cried. "Now after having him, I can't live without him. What am I gonna do? He never even knew about—about the baby…" The girl dwarfed Margie's tiny frame as she went limp in her arms and wailed.

When the initial shock and anguish passed, Mary was exhausted and Margie let her slowly collapse down on the sofa, propping a pillow under her head and covering her with an afghan. She made a fresh pot of coffee and eased quietly into her chair to light a cigarette. Looking up, she whispered to God. "God, I don't pretend to understand you or have the right to question you, but I don't know why you let this happen. These two kids had a chance to be real happy. You know what my Mary's life has been like, better than I do. You know she deserves to be happy. Please help her now. Amen." She rubbed her forehead and took a draw on the cigarette, shook her head in resignation and tapped an ash into the ashtray. It was 8:30 a.m. and it was going to be a long, hard day.

****

That day was easy compared to the day of the funeral. In the morning, people from the restaurant stopped by with food and desserts. Mary was sorely tempted to hole up in her room and avoid them, but she knew it was unfair to let it all fall on her mom. They were only trying to be nice, after all. Even Sandy brought a casserole and hugged Mary, telling her that she would be at the service. When ol' Chet came by, his head hung down and handed her a large tray of deli meats, so sympathetic that he didn't know what to say, it almost made her cry.

Mary and her mother sat expressionless before the flag-draped coffin in the church, as the organist played softly and people filed in the back door and were seated. Not that they had that many friends, but people from the Crab House and several neighbors of Margie's managed to fill six rows of pews. Jimmy's parents sat speechless in the second pew, his mother reaching up to squeeze Mary's shoulder whispering encouragement. There were even a few military personnel, and Mary would find out later that they were men and women who had become acquainted with Jimmy on the ship. Dressed in black with her hair up, the young widow had none of the luster of the joyful bride and newlywed that was hers a few months earlier.

After a brief service, the military pallbearers escorted the casket to the hearse for the short drive to Northbeach Cemetery. Mary stood stoically as the committal service was held and the military paid its final honors. Then, it all was over. And as hard as it was, it didn't seem like it was long enough. The flag that had draped his coffin was neatly folded into a triangle and presented to Mary. As the mourners padded back across the green grass to their cars, Margie left her daughter alone beside the casket suspended over the grave.

Oh, Jimmy, Mary thought. Why didn't you come along about five, ten or fifteen years sooner? We should have had more time together. Why did I distrust you? Damn, why did I put you off for so long? I was such an idiot. Why did I have to be such a bitch to you? All those weeks you tried to get me to date you, we could have been together but I wasted them all. She felt her stomach. You never even knew that we were going to have a baby. I don't know how I'm gonna make it without you. After being so happy, how do I go back to the way my life was before you? When will my heart begin to believe that you're really gone?

She bent over and kissed the cold casket, then threw herself across it, wailing with grief. Finally releasing all her pent-up sorrow and the grief in her heart, her tears fell upon the top of the cold, metal vault. It was a final goodbye to her precious Jimmy, and it was as though the floodgates of her broken heart opened up and poured out every ounce of her anguish and heartache. She didn't want to leave him there. She didn't want to leave him out there in the approaching darkness. She didn't want them to put him into the ground, all alone down there through the cold, lonely night. She stood up, picked up a white rose and laid it on the casket and managed to whisper breathlessly, "I love you, hon." Even knowing that her husband lay lifeless in the coffin, as she turned and walked away, she felt like she was abandoning him there in

THEY NEVER REALLY LEAVE

the cemetery.

****

At the Air Force hospital in Weisbadden, Germany, the patient identified as Rod Nelson was in critical condition, with second-degree burns over 50 percent of his body, multiple shrapnel wounds and a head injury that had required neurosurgery. Mr. and Mrs. Michael Nelson arrived at 7:30 a.m. local time that morning and rushed to the hospital. It was an older military hospital, with discolored-tiled walls and poor lighting in the corridors. When they were led into the room where their son was being cared for, Mrs. Nelson nearly fainted. Covered in gauze from head to toe, tubes were coming from everywhere on her son.

In no way prepared for what they would see, Monika Nelson steadied herself against her husband as they watched the nurses tending to the bevy of i.v.'s, chest tubes and other drainage devices attached to Rod. The only motion from his body was the rhythmic up and down movement of his chest as the tracheostomy tube and ventilator breathed for him. Michael was less fortunate than his wife; he promptly vomited in the waste can near the bed from the pungent odor of burnt flesh and medical ointments.

"Oh God, I'm sorry," he apologized.

"Think nothing of it, sir," the orderly consoled him as he pulled a chair for Mrs. Nelson. He picked up the trashcan to clean it. "Happens to everyone." He left for a moment, returned with a face cloth, towel, and small bar of soap, and gave Michael directions to the public restroom.

"Rod," she gasped as she sat down, clutching her hands to her chest. "Oh, Rod honey. I'm so sorry." Her mind raced back to her son's bout with pneumonia when he was six. She'd fidgeted in a chair beside his hospital bed all night, watching him breathe, praying that his lungs would clear. He was so tiny, so frail back then. She'd also insisted that she be allowed to stay overnight even though the doctor said the boy was doing much better. Her only child was her whole life, and she guarded him as such.

He was still her only child. Still the apple of her eye. Even when he teased her at the holidays about hovering and doting over him, she'd smile widely and deny the whole thing. Her husband Michael had become accustomed over the years to playing second fiddle to his son, but truth be known, he felt the same way about Rod that Monika did.

"The doctor will be making his rounds in about and hour. You can speak to him about your son then, if you like," the nurse said.

"Thank you," Monika Nelson managed.

"Maybe we should get some air," Michael motioned for the door.

"No, that's okay. You go ahead. I want to stay here, with my son," she answered.

"Our son. You sure about that?" Want me to bring you anything? Coffee?"

"Yeah, sure. Coffee would be nice. Thanks." She didn't take her eyes off of Rod. Her son. Her only child, the apple of her eye. Why'd she let him enlist in this damned Navy anyways?

It took Michael Nelson the better part of forty-five minutes just to find the cafeteria and make it back to Rod's room. Just as he expected, he found his wife still seated beside their son, her head bowed in prayer. Her cheeks were wet from sobbing and even her handkerchief was soaked in the mother's tears. She startled and looked up with red eyes as her husband spoke.

"Jeeze, sorry it took so long, I got all turned around trying to get back to this room." He handed her the tepid coffee and she sat it on the windowsill. It was the last thing she was concerned about right now. "I wonder when that doctor is going to make it in here—it's already 10:30."

"Soon, I hope. I can hardly stand it—not one of these nurses will talk to me about Rodney's condition. They keep saying the doctor will discuss it with us. Why do they have to be so secretive?" Her husband shrugged his shoulders and leaned against the wall to sip his coffee. She shot daggers at him from her eyes. "And I for the life of me cannot understand how you can be so lackadaisical—out wandering the halls looking for the cafeteria to get coffee. For God's sake, Michael, our son is laying here barely alive!"

The man erupted. "Lackadaisical? You think I don't care our boy is lying here half dead? What the hell are you thinking? I'd gladly trade places with him if I could. You know that. Damn! You make me crazy sometimes woman." She sniffed her disapproval and moved her gaze back to her son. There wasn't another word between the two of them for forty-five minutes, when the doctor arrived.

"Doctor, thank heavens you're here. We're his parents. How's he doing?"

He shook their hands. "Mr. Nelson, Mrs. Nelson. I'm Doctor Aiken. Your son is in very serious but stable condition. He has received second-degree burns over 55% of his body, and had some other major shrapnel wounds. What concerns us now beside the burns is a head injury he received as well."

The parents exchanged glances, and she said, "A head injury. Was it severe?"

"I'm afraid so. After he arrived here yesterday, we stabilized him and took him directly to surgery."

Michael Nelson was astonished. "You mean, he had brain surgery?"

"Yes. We had to go in to relieve the pressure from the swelling of his brain, and when we got in there, we discovered significant bleeding and tissue damage."

Monika Nelson held her hand to her mouth as her eyes widened. "You mean that he's had—"

"Brain damage. It's possible, yes. To what extent we won't know until he regains consciousness, that is, if he does. I don't believe in giving people false hope—he's been injured badly." He flipped through the chart and read a few nurse's notes. "He's held on this long, folks. The next 48 hours will give us a better idea if he's even going to survive. As you see, he's not even breathing on his own yet. I wish I had better news for you." He started to leave the room and Monika motioned wildly for him to stay.

"Wait, doctor. This is all happening so fast. I have so many questions. When will he wake up?"

"There's no way of knowing that, Mrs. Nelson. It could be days, weeks or months."

"Oh my God, months?" She began sobbing violently and her husband rushed to console her. She pulled away from him as her concern for her son overwhelmed her.

"Come on, honey. You know Rod's a tough kid. If anyone can make it through this, he can. He will come through it." Monika Nelson put her face in her lap and wept.

"Thank you doctor for filling us in," Michael said.

"I'll see you later today or tomorrow," Doctor Aiken said as he slipped out the door.

She steely glared and pointed a finger of fury at her husband. "You. You had to go and encourage him to enlist in the Navy. Just because you did and your father did. He would be getting ready for the first semester of his junior year of college right now instead of laying here in this bed. Get out of my sight."

Michael expected this, but the magnitude of her blame still shocked him. "Honey, we're both tired from the flight. I think if you'll—"

"Get the hell out of here!" She screamed. A linebacker of a nurse was passing by the room and heard the shouting.

"Excuse me, folks. This is a hospital. And your son is not the only patient trying to get well here. You're going to have to quiet down or leave."

"Leave. Right now," Monika said under her voice, glowering at her husband. The nurse waited to see what was going to happen next.

"Okay, okay. I'll go back to the motel room." He pulled a slip of paper from his pocket. "Here's the phone number if you want me to come get you. You really should come along and get some rest, dear."

"I'm staying right here." He gave the nurse a defeated look and they both left.

****

Although Mary vehemently denied that it was necessary, Margie insisted on moving in for a few weeks after the funeral. There was a scant distance between their two homes, but she just had a notion to do so. And although there were many changes she and her daughter were going through, Margie could still be stubborn as a mule.

Most days Mary had no interest in going out in public, shopping or to get her hair done, so Margie would do the marketing and go to the post office, even wash Mary's hair for her under the kitchen sink like she used to when she was a little girl. She'd tenderly dry the wavy scarlet hair and brush it as they talked. But Mary's gloomy mood tarried and it became clear to her mother that she would need counseling if she were ever to go back to a normal life again. The biggest hurdle was how to convince her.

"Mary, honey, would you go if I called and made an appointment for you to talk to one of the grief counselors down at the clinic? Judith Earle at the hairdresser's shop says that they helped her aunt a lot when she lost her husband."

Mary whirled around, knocking the hairbrush out of Margie's hand. "What? You want me to do what?" Her face darkened like a noreaster. "Mother, I don't want you talking about me at the beauty shop. Just who do you think you are telling me what I need? I don't need to go to no damned counselor. What I need is my husband back! What I need is my life back!"

"I know, baby, but—"

"I'm not your baby. If you're gonna start stickin' your nose in where it don't belong, you can pack your bags right now and go home. Maybe I'm not handling this as well as I should. Maybe it's going to take a lot of time. One damn thing I know is I had everything—now I have nothing. Tell me, mother, just how long should it take you to get over that?"

"I don't know," Margie turned away and leaned against the kitchen counter, looking out the small window over the sink at the sunny day outside. "I don't know, honey. But I've been sober for over three weeks now, and I've seen you get worse as I get better. I really want you to see a counselor. You've been through so much."

Mary was in her mother's face immediately, "You will mind your own business or get out of my life. Now that's the damned end of it, do you hear me?" She stormed to her bedroom and slammed the door.

Margie would've given her right arm for a shot of Jack Daniels, but instead put on her coat and headed down the street to her AA meeting.

Distancing herself from her mother for the time being, Mary began to find some solace in long walks along the shore in early morning. She'd rise at 5:00 a.m. before her mother and quietly slip out the door. The cool, wet sand under her feet and the gentle, foamy brine of the surf felt good, and she smiled as she looked behind, seeing her footprints in the sand being abruptly erased by the failing tide. Just like Jimmy. There he was, for a moment, the answer to everything she ever hoped for. The one man that she finally gave her heart and soul to, there he was, and then there he wasn't. The impressions her feet made in the sand—the impressions his love had written on her heart. All washed away now, as though they were never there. As the sun peeked over the azure horizon of the sea, the breakers glistened and shone as they gyrated. A flock of pelicans, like an air squadron in formation skimmed the waves and rode the air current as they soared south for the day.

The day the letter came from the Department of the Navy, Mary was on her way out the door for work when her mother handed her the envelope. It was from the Commander of the Atlantic fleet. "Dear Mrs. Gallant, it was our earnest desire to provide you with your husband's remains in an expeditious manner, in order that you and your family could honor him with a memorial service and burial. Unfortunately, during the retrieval of bodies from the burning Forrestal, Boatswain's Mate Gallant's identification tags were disassociated from the body and in the massive confusion caused by the catastrophe, we fear that there could have been an error made. However, it is entirely possible that the remains that were rendered to you were in fact your husband.

We have launched a detailed investigation and a local Naval officer will be contacting you to discuss possible disinterment of the body. Be assured that the Department of the Navy is doing everything it can to resolve this, and we regret the discomfort and anxiousness it will surely cause you."

Sincerely,

James V. Summerfield, Commander Atlantic Fleet

"Damnit! Damnit, Mother! I can't believe these assholes!" She

THEY NEVER REALLY LEAVE

flung the letter at her mother and sat down at the kitchen table. As Margie read, her eyes reflected the horror and disbelief of her daughter's. "Oh my God, mom, they don't even know if that was Jimmy in the casket! How can they be so stupid? This is just too damned much. They send me a body and let me grieve over it and then they decide it's the wrong person? I have to get out of here."

"Where're ya gonna go, Mary?" her mother's eyes were pools of tears.

"I don't know—yes, I do. I'm going down to the personnel office at the shipyard. I'm gonna shove this paper in their face and tell them what I think. Call Chet and tell him I'll be in late, mom. This is the craziest damned thing I ever heard of, and I'm going down there to raise some hell. They won't know what hit them."

"Mary, I—" she was cut off as the door slammed behind her daughter as she sailed out the door, on her way to make some unlucky officer grow a few more gray hairs.

Without a word, Mary handed the young man behind the desk at the Norfolk Naval Shipyard office the letter and waited for a response. No matter what his reaction, she was willing and ready to tear into him with a tongue lashing like he'd never had before. In a particularly astute moment of good judgment, Yeoman Perez quickly escorted her to a private conference room where he directed her to sit at a long table with heavy, cold uncomfortable metal chairs. He assured her that someone would be with her as soon as possible. She pulled one of the arctic chairs up to the table and check her watch. 2:30. We'll see how soon "possible" is, she thought.

The room was desolate aside from the table and the ten chairs that lined it, no pictures on the walls, not even any ship memorabilia or Navy insignias. She unfolded the letter and read it again, and she was sure that she could feel her blood pressure rising to the point of bursting every pulsing artery and vein in her body. It was so quiet behind the closed steel door that she could hear her rapid heart beat. Wiping the sweat from her forehead, she sat up straighter in the chair and closed the letter.

If the person she buried wasn't Jimmy, then where was he? No, she couldn't let herself do that. She couldn't get her hopes up that he could still be alive somewhere. So they'd found his tags. What does that prove-he could have dropped those anywhere. Mary was trying to keep her composure, but her mind was racing through the possibilities. Where is that guy? It's 3 p.m. already. She wrung her hands, reaching into her pocketbook for the photo of the two of them that the J.P. in Norfolk had his wife take on the night they were married. Happiness seemed so distant now. How do you go on, when everything you ever dreamed of finally comes and is suddenly taken away from you?

That first night together in the bridal suite of the fanciest hotel in Richmond, making love and holding each other so tight, was a memory that would have to sustain her over the tough years ahead. I knew it was too good to be true, she thought. The whole time, feeling like Cinderella with my prince; I knew I didn't deserve it. But feeling Jimmy's arms encircling her, his warm breath against her bare neck, the tender kisses he lavished on her, she'd forced herself to put aside all the feelings of unworthiness to savor every moment of it.

It was 3:30 and Mary'd had enough of the waiting. She walked to the door, opened it and bellowed out to the kid at the counter, "Hey, you there. Remember me? Is anyone coming to talk to me or not?"

"Uh, yes m'am." He looked across the busy office nervously. "I'll remind them again that you're waiting. I'm sure they'll be right in." She frowned and slipped back in the door, leaving it half open.

At 4:15 two men entered the room where Mary was waiting. One, the short fat guy, she recognized as a Chief Petty Officer and the other was a tall black man dressed in an officer's uniform. The Chief spoke up first. "Sorry to keep you waiting, Mrs.—uh—Gallant. It was unavoidable. I'm Chief Powell and this is Lieutenant Commander Dietz."

They both took seats near her and opened some files they carried. The Lieutenant spoke next.

"We are greatly saddened and concerned about the confusion over the remains of your late husband, Petty Officer Gallant. Our records show that he was an outstanding member of the armed forces and served his country proudly. Please accept our condolences in your loss. Now, in the letter that you received—"

"In the letter I received it said I may have buried the wrong person," she snapped.

"Yes, m'am. We have a copy of that communication." The lieutenant pulled at his collar, trying to loosen it. "As you no doubt have heard on the news, the awful conflagration aboard the Forrestal made it difficult and chaotic to retrieve the dead and wounded. Frankly, in some cases, there just wasn't much left of some of the poor souls who were lost that day. I don't think you want me to get any more graphic than that. If there was any error made in the remains that were returned to you, it would indeed be a grievous error, but not an impossible one."

Mary leaned over the table, looking him straight in the eye. "So is there a possibility that my husband could be alive out there somewhere?"

"Quite frankly, no. Roll calls were taken and people accounted for, and his military-issue dog tags were found on the flight deck beside his body."

"Then why the hell was I sent this letter?"

The chief spoke up. "We just don't know, Mrs. Gallant. The investigating officers must have come across something that caught their eye and they want to confirm the identity of your husband's body."

"And how are they gonna do that? Go dig him up and run a test?"

"M'am, we've just received this letter as you have. Before you go getting all upset that the body will have to be exhumed, let us do some checking to find out what they plan to do about it. I can assure you that the Navy will do everything in its power to prevent you from any further grief than you've already had to bear. We can tell you also that none of this will be made public knowledge for now, and we ask that you not speak to the newspapers about it either. It could only—uh—hamper the investigation."

"Oh, don't worry about that. I don't want this broadcast any more than you do. But let me tell you something right now—I demand that you call me with any news as soon as you get it—and I don't want you avoiding my phone calls, because believe me, I'll be right back down here in your faces again. I know all about how you military officials give people the runaround. And I'm not takin' any of your crap—understand?"

The lieutenant stood, "Mrs. Gallant, as soon as we know something more, we'll let you know. That's the best we can do. We're very sorry for all of this."

She sniffed her disapproval, gave them both a doubtful look and the chief ushered her out of the conference room and down the hall to the door leading to the parking lot.

Chapter 12

Mary was working as many shifts at the Crab House as she could get lately. The numbing effect of losing Jimmy and the baby all at once had made the inept tourists downright tolerable. And the more hours she put in there, the less she'd have to sit in her apartment watching television reports and waiting for the phone to ring. The hopeless, empty feeling hung over her and clouded her judgment. She couldn't escape it. She couldn't get under it, or over it or around it, so she resigned to herself that she had to go through it.

Her mother moved back home, finally. Mary was glad that she was getting her life straightened around at long last, but after she stopped drinking it was like she thought she had the answers to all of life's problems. She was really starting to annoy Mary with the counseling idea.

After Margie went home, Mary decided that there was way too little of Jimmy in the apartment. There was the bed and the kitchen table that they picked out together, two places that she spent a lot of time at. And there are his clothes hanging in the closet that she loved to visit daily. There was the dark blue pinstripe suit he wore the night they'd gotten married that she would lay out on their bed and smell his faint, sweet cologne but she'd always end up bawling for an hour afterward. But they hadn't lived there long enough to even have little mementos and souvenirs or trinkets that they'd gotten together.

One morning, an idea came to her. She pulled out the pictures they'd taken at the Justice of the Peace and his parents' house and plastered them all over the side of the fridge. Now there was more of him there.

****

Mary continued on this bend, cutting out words and pictures and landscapes from magazines and newspapers and making collages of all sizes to cover the bare walls of the apartment. It became an obsession to her, but it was an outlet for her grief. Margie stopped by one day about a week into the project and was dumbfounded at the display.

"Mare, what's all this?"

"All what, mother?"

"All these faces and buildings and trees and words and stuff you've put all over your walls?"

"They're called collages, mother."

"I know what they're called girl, but why are you doing this?" She traced the outline of a palm tree along a beach on the wall. The subtitle under it read "Paradise."

"You couldn't possibly understand if I told you, so why bother." Mary pointed to the coffeepot. "Have some coffee?"

Each week when her mother stopped by, Mary had new artwork adorning her walls. When she ran out of room in the kitchen and living room, she started down the hall and into the bedroom and bathroom. Some displays were disturbing, pictures of the burning Forrestal with the headline of the New York Times, "Disaster at Sea; Navy says over 100 sailors lost." There were Navy photos of the dead servicemen, including Jimmy, that she'd cut out and put some in the air over the burning ship, some in other pictures like the palm tree on the beach. Another face appeared pasted over a picture of a boy and his golden retriever puppy. Sometimes it looked like she was trying to make the men live on, under the palm tree or as the little boy. Words like "horrendous," "unspeakable," "bloody" had been cut out and pasted next to pictures. Sometimes a face would appear in a photographer's shot of a fire in a building. And there were babies everywhere—babies smiling, babies laughing, babies crying. Margie knew all along that her daughter was in deep trouble, but until she saw the morbid vignettes she hoped that Mary would snap out of it eventually. As for Jimmy's picture from the newspaper, it was used in the most puzzling way yet. She had found a strikingly beautiful photograph of a monarch butterfly and pasted his head on it.

"Mary, why is Jimmy's head on this moth?" Margie asked.

"It's not a moth, Mom. It's a beautiful butterfly."

"Okay, so it's a beautiful butterfly. Why is his head on it?"

"Oh crap, mother—I told you that you wouldn't understand these things. A butterfly is a symbol of eternal life, didn't you ever know that?"

"Apparently not," the wounded woman replied. She stared at Jimmy's metamorphosis for a few moments, choosing her words carefully and sighed. "Mary, it's time you got some help. I know we've argued about it, but you are not doing good. This-these things-are not good."

Mary thrust her palms out and leaned against the wall. "Don't start that with me again, Mom."

"I wouldn't be your mother if I didn't care enough to tell you the truth. Damnit girl, you gotta get help! You're crackin' up!" The woman's voice was unsteady and her hands were gyrating as she spoke. Margie had become a nervous wreck worrying about her daughter, but Mary couldn't see it.

"Oh please. Save the drama for your AA meetings, Mother. I'm doing just fine, if it bothers you to see these things, stop coming around. I've been waiting for three long weeks since the Navy sent me that letter saying that I might have buried the wrong man. I've been able to channel some of my grief and pain into these montages. Why are you always questioning me, like I'm still a child? I'm so sick of hearing you whine about what you think and how you worry. Can't you start concentrating on Frankie and leave me alone?"

"Frankie stopped coming around a month ago."

"Oh, I see. About the time you quit drinkin', right?"

"Yeah I guess so."

"What a scumbag. I told you he was a loser."

"Yeah, but I was always too drunk to listen. I might be coming around a lot less, I signed up for this real estate course they're giving at the community college."

"What for?"

"To sell houses, dummy. Whaddya think for? Anyways, it's evening classes and eight weeks long. After it's over we have to take the state exam to get our licenses and then they say they'll help us get into a realtor's office. So? Whaddya think?"

Mary beamed. "I think it's terrific, mom. I really do."

"Okay, good then." Margie said, relieved. It was the nicest thing Mary had said to her in weeks. Maybe her daughter was going to make it through this. At least it was the first recognizable glimpse of the "old" Mary.

The next morning Mary set out for her beach walk as always, barefoot in her rolled-up jeans and oversized t-shirt and a white sweater. She had her hair pulled back with a scarf. The ocean was placid, licking at the shore playfully as the cool morning tide encircled the woman's ankles. For as far as Mary could see, there were no clouds, only the bluest of blue skies. The smell of the ocean seemed new to her today. Something was different. She couldn't put a finger on it, but in her innermost being, something was beginning to stir. The other early risers she passed all smiled and spoke and it didn't annoy her. Walkers and joggers passed her by in both directions, nodding and grinning at her as though they knew a secret.

The huge, blazing sun crept higher above the horizon and Mary took off her sweatshirt and tied it around her shoulders. A billion shimmering prisms of light reflected in the azure sea as the sun announced the dawning of a new day. Oh, Jimmy, she thought. If only you were here right now to see this beautiful day. Where are you? Do I dare hope that you're out there somewhere, alive? Damn this military for getting my hopes up! I don't know what to do! This is hell waiting for them to get this straightened out. Utterly hell. Waiting and waiting. You'd know what to do, darling. If the tables were turned, what would you do? That question stopped her in her tracks, and suddenly the sky opened up and she knew exactly what she needed to do.

Ah, the bliss of an epiphany. Mary spun around to race for home and smack! was knocked flat on her back by a jogger. "Oh my gosh, I'm sorry. Are you hurt?" The young man was leaning over her in the sun, dazed and not quite sure himself what had happened.

"I—I'm okay. It was my fault," she said. She squinted but couldn't see him in the sun, but the voice sounded familiar. As he helped her to her feet, she remembered. "Doctor Boyer? Is that you?"

"Uh, yes. I'm Michael Boyer. Do we know one another?"

"You took care of me a few months back. I was in the hospital after being attacked. Mary Gallant. Don't you remember me?"

The handsome young man looked puzzled, but then he remembered. "Of course. How have you been doing? You never came back for your follow up visit, you know. I had my nurse leave a message with your mother at your home."

She felt stupid and guilty as she gazed into his puppy-dog brown eyes. "Hmm. She must have forgotten to tell me. Sorry." Suddenly everything was awkward and she wanted to bolt.

"Are you sure you're okay, Mrs. Gallant?" She never would have guessed the athletic body that was hidden beneath the scrubs he wore at the hospital. She felt ashamed even looking at him, but he had been so nice to her. And he was the only person besides Jimmy who made her feel safe when she was with him.

"Yeah, I'm fine. Thanks, Doctor Boyer."

"You really should call the office for a followup examination."

"Okay, I'll do that right away. Thanks again." She smiled as he turned and waved to continue his run down the beach.

When the doctor had disappeared down the beach, Mary hightailed it for home. She quickly recovered despite her ogling indulgence and had much more to do than the time to plan it in. At last she knew what needed to be done.

****

Mary was quickly waved on as she flashed her dependent's i.d. card at the guard gate at the Naval Medical Center in Portsmouth. Her growing doubts about the reliability of the Navy's report of her husband's death were coming to a head as she parked the car and headed toward the north wing of the building. News reports had mentioned that, after being transferred from a military hospital in Germany, the wounded from the Forrestal accident were being taken to two hospitals; Portsmouth, Virginia and San Diego, California. With Portsmouth only a 35-minute drive from home, she could've kicked herself for not thinking of it sooner.

The Elizabeth River glistened lazily in the sun as she walked toward the beige brick building, the skyline of Norfolk looming across the river where only a few months earlier she and Jimmy had exchanged vows. A gust of wind off the river tossed her scarlet hair and she pulled it to the side of her face to gaze over at the city, unsure whether she wanted to scream or cry. She lingered there a moment and went on her way.

"What was the last name again, m'am?" the nurse behind the counter asked.

"Gallant. James Gallant."

"No, I'm sorry, he's not a patient at this hospital." The nurse looked over her glasses at Mary and straightened her starched white top. "Weren't you notified of where he was taken?"

Mary fibbed. "Uh, yeah. But my mom took the message and truth is she, uh, drinks sometimes…"

"Oh, I see." She adjusted her thick eyeglasses and squinted as she scrutinized the tall redhead, dressed a bit provocatively for her puritanical tastes in a red halter top and low-cut bellbottom jeans. "But you should also have received written communication about your husband's whereabouts." She had her there.

Ignoring the last point, Mary said "so I was sure he'd have been brought here to Portsmouth, since Norfolk is the Forrestal's home port and we live in Virginia Beach. Could you please check the list again?" Mary leaned over the counter more to read the list of names upside down. The nurse quickly flipped the report over and glared.

"Well, Mrs. Gallant, if he was here, he'd be listed on this patient roster." She was the quintessential know-it-all bitch nurse. She sat back in her chair and folded her arms. Case closed, as far as she was concerned. "I suggest you contact the medical center in San Diego."

"But there could be some mistake…"

"I'm afraid the mistake was yours, M'am." Maybe she was having a bad day.

"But reports can be wrong sometimes, can't they? I mean, how many injured have you been getting in here every day?"

"Plenty. But our hospital census reports are cross-checked with the new admissions twice a day, so you see it's not possible that there'd be a mistake."

"Dammit, don't tell me that's not possible! I've seen how the military can screw things up firsthand," Mary slammed a fist on the cracked, aging counter.

The older woman stared her down. "Please lower your voice. I understand how important it is that you find your husband. I'm afraid you've just come to the wrong place. Have you spoken with the Command center at the base?"

The redhead was just getting started. Glancing at the nurse's name badge, she said, "look here, Lieutenant Kipfer, I've been to the Ombudsman's office, I've been to the Command center, I've called the Bureau of Naval Personnel, I've called the ship every other day, I've called everyone I can think of to call. Hell, I've even called Washington. Everyone keeps giving me the runaround. Now are you going to take me through your wards so I can look for my husband or am I going to have to make a bigger stink to get this done? Get this straight, lady, I will go to whatever lengths it takes in order to find him. Who's the C.O. of this hospital?"

"Captain Barrymore, but he's not…"

"Okay, tell me what floor his office is on, please."

"But—" The Lieutenant was new at this command, and didn't want her first experience with the Commanding Officer to be on a negative note. She glanced over her shoulder and saw Lieutenant Commander Stanton at the medication cart. "Hold on for just a moment, please. I'll be right back." She pushed her chair away from the counter, and dashed back to her co-worker to recant the dilemma she was facing. Mary couldn't hear what they were saying but the higher-ranking officer was glancing at her and then the other nurse and shaking her head.

Thinking that she was about to be turned away, she bolted for the door to the ward and pushed her way through. The acrid odor of infected wounds, burns and death stung in her nostrils. Along both sides of the long ward were hospital beds practically stacked upon each other, with injured and dying men struggling to stay alive, some moaning incessantly, some screaming out in pain at times. Many had several sizes of tubes going in and coming out of them and some had machines breathing for them. One poor soul lay staring at the ceiling, both his hands and face burned and the bandaged stumps of what used to be his legs elevated on pillows. Another sat on the edge of his bed, using a urinal under the sheet, his head wrapped in gauze except for his right eye. His hospital gown was open in the back and Mary shuddered at the hideous sight. The skin from his waist up was burned badly, some charred black and some bloody red and oozing onto the sheet. He turned when he saw her coming and whistled. "Whoo-hoo, boys. The nurses are gettin' better lookin' all the time!" Mary smiled to hide her revulsion.

"Mrs. Gallant! How dare you come into my medical ward without permission?" Uh-oh. Lieutenant Kipfer was on her in a split second, grasping Mary by the shoulders to turn her around.

"Let go of me! I'm not leaving, you hear? You can call the MP's if you want to, but they'll have to haul me out of here. You hear me?" She lowered her voice and peered deeper into the nurse's eyes, shooting daggers. "And I'll go kicking and screaming the whole way, and the whole command here will know what you did to me, and every newspaper and radio in Norfolk and Virginia Beach will, too."

The nurse motioned with her hands for Mary to quiet down. "Mrs. Gallant, I was coming to tell you that we've decided to take you through our wards. But you cannot just waltz through here unescorted. A corpsman will accompany you. You know we have five floors with patients on them, with three wards on each floor. This is going to take you more than a few hours."

Mary regrouped for a moment, then threw her hands up in the air and said, "When do we start?"

****

I was told to come back tomorrow, Tuesday, when a corpsman would be available for the entire day to take me through the hospital. That night I barely slept. I kept thinking about Jimmy, lying there injured and in horrific pain, unable to move or speak. I thought about his sweet blue eyes and that mischievous half-smile he always gave me when he was up to something. Oh God, please let him be all right!

I remembered the day when he told me that he believed that all his life had been leading up to the point of meeting me, and that now he was complete. I wondered if I made him know that I felt the same about him. I tried to remember how many times I told him that I loved him. I searched and I searched my memory for the unforgettable, savory, tender lovemaking we'd made and asked myself if I'd done enough to make him feel special. To make him feel like a man that was loved.

****

Through the warm summer night, I tiptoed barefoot in the moonlight through a dew-covered verdant garden in the woods, smelling the musk of the composting leaves and looking there and here for my love. Behind the tree, no; around that rock, no. But he must be here, he told me he would always be here. Here in our private, secret place. Amidst the lacy ferns, rock moss and wildflowers; white and lavender-colored wild phlox, jack-in-the-pulpits perched stately beneath their cathedral-ceiling leaves, and snow-white trillium; among the chirping crickets and birds of the night. Where is he?

I cannot find him. I should feel alarmed, yet a subtle peacefulness has swept over me and I know in my heart that I will find him. I cannot grow weary in my searching; I must not become complacent or disheartened. He is out there, somewhere. I feel him all around me. Heaven help me, am I awake or dreaming?

****

After my dream, I tossed and turned for hours, and morning finally came so I leapt out of bed to take a quick shower and dress. I wore a light blue sweater and a pair of jeans and tied my hair back. I drove out of Virginia Beach into Norfolk and was entering the tunnel at 7:30 when my oil light came on. Just my luck, I thought. A quick stop at a service station and the attendant added a quart of oil and told me I should be set to go.

I passed through the checkpoint at the gate and pulled into a visitor's parking space. With the engine still running, I was suddenly jarred by emotions that I'd been trying to suppress and hide. I felt like putting the car into drive and taking off. I couldn't stand not knowing the truth about Jimmy—now I wondered if I could stand knowing it.

What shape would I find him in when I found him?

Damn! Jimmy, you always brought out the best (and worst) in me. I felt my heart racing and there was a sickly, foreboding feeling in my stomach.

After a couple of minutes I was okay and I shut the motor off and got out of the car. The corpsman who was supposed to usher me around the wards didn't come on duty until 8:00 a.m., so my new "friend," Lieutenant Kipfer suggested I go down to the cafeteria for coffee and she would send him down when he arrived.

"Mrs. Gallant? I'm Petty Officer Jim Petersen." A tall, slender blond boy dressed in a crisp white uniform stood before me. Smooth shaven and very clean cut, he looked like a junior high school student. He smiled, but his hazel eyes were sympathetic and rather shy.

Believe me when I tell you that I would never be unfaithful to my Jimmy. He means the whole world to me, he opened up a new world to me. I was embittered against men for so long before I met him, but after a few weeks with him I found out what it can be like to be treated like a lady by a man who loves you. I started to notice handsome men again. Like that Doctor Boyer. Jimmy awakened all my senses, including a new appreciation for members of the opposite sex. That's all there is to it.

So this young corpsman, Petty Officer Petersen took me to the second floor of the hospital and we began the arduous task of going bed to bed, trying to identify Jimmy. I saw more suffering and sadness than I could fit into a lifetime that day. There was every type of injury you could think of from the accident, Petersen told me. More than once I had to pause and take a few moments before entering another putrid, foul-smelling ward. Some men could get up out of bed while others were so badly injured and burned that they were immobile, wrapped in yards of gauze that oozed with serum and ointments. Many were unconscious, had their faces completely wrapped, and were attached to breathing machines, and I stopped at each and gazed down, trying in vain to find Jimmy somewhere beneath the bandages and tubes.

It was all too much, even for a tough old bird like me. I thanked Petty Officer Petersen at the end of the day and fled the hospital, bawling like a baby all the way to my car.

When I made it home, I put some coffee on and called mother to come over. I needed someone to talk to. She was there in six minutes and we sat down in the living room.

"Oh, Mom, it was so horrible. All those men. In so much pain. Some missing limbs, some with terrible burns, some unconscious, not even breathing on their own."

"Yeah, I figured it was gonna be pretty tough on ya, kid. But you made it through it, didn't you?" She tapped her pack of camels and pulled one out and lit it.

"Yeah, just barely though. I made a list of the names and locations of the ones who could possibly be Jimmy."

"What? What d'ya mean, could be Jimmy?"

I was tired and suddenly felt less than patient with my mother. "Mother, many of them were unconscious and all bandaged up. I couldn't even see their faces. A lot of them were on those breathing machines too."

"I still don't see how you could guess—"

I leaned forward. "I could guess because maybe their height or weight was like Jimmy's, or an arm or hand looked like his."

Mom flicked an ash into the ashtray. "You must've been there a while."

"I was—all day."

There was a long, silent pause while I sat looking toward the window, the Atlantic and the sky above it becoming grayer and darker with the setting of the sun. Mom smoked her cigarette and contemplated her daughter's actions. She knew I was strong-willed, but this went well beyond anything she'd have guessed me to do. Well, no it wasn't. Not really.

"So what're you gonna do now, Mary?" Mom said as she ground out her smoke and her brow furrowed, waiting for an answer.

"I guess I'm going to California."

Chapter 13

"Monika. Monika, wake up." The woman startled from her sleep and looked at her husband bleary-eyed.

"What is it, Michael?"

"It's 7:00 a.m. and you've been in this room all night," he said, sounding like a father. I want you to go to the motel and get at least a couple hours of good sleep—in a bed." Monika Nelson stretched in the chair and rubbed her eyes. Touching her son's hand, she smiled at her concerned husband.

"I'm sorry about the way I talked to you last night, honey. You were right—we were both tired and I said a lot of things that I didn't mean. I realized as soon as you left how stupid I'd been."

Michael grinned and rubbed the back of his wife's neck. "Don't worry about it. Now will you take my advice and let me take over here for a few hours?"

Hesitantly, she answered, "Yeah, all right. But if there's any change, anything at all, call me. I mean it, Mike. Promise?"

"I promise," he said. With that, Monika stood and walked to the window, admiring the panoramic Weisbadden sunrise.

"What a beautiful morning," she marveled. "If only Rod could see it." Michael Nelson said nothing. She put on her jacket, kissed his cheek and slipped out the door.

Mike looked at the clock. 7:15 a.m. For a long time, he avoided looking directly at his son in the bed that morning. He noted the gray-white walls of the room and the yellowed over-waxed tiles on the floor. The ceiling tiles were loose in some spots, and the flourescent lights overhead had a bulb going. He rose from the chair and watched from the window as traffic sputtered by on the small brick avenue outside. Monnie was right. It was a beautiful morning outside of this room. Inside, it was dreadfully gloomy and the pungent odors in the room were coming from his son.

She was right. He pushed Rod to sign up for the Navy. But who knows when his draft number would have come up anyway? At least in the Navy, Michael thought his son might be stationed on a ship, safely away from hand-to-hand combat. He promised himself that he would never interfere in his son's life again. Whatever life his son was going to have after this, that is.

That's when it happened. He whirled about, forcing himself to look at his son. The oozing bandages covered his head and face, both arms and down his neck to his waist. Tubes were going in, i.v.'s and a nasal-gastric drain, feeding tubes filled with wheat-colored liquid and the breathing tubes, of course. Chest tubes that were a half inch in diameter carried fluid and blood away from his chest, and smaller drains were drawing crimson streams of blood from his head. The room began to spin around Michael Nelson and everything became pitch black. He would later remember only a painful thud! as his forehead hit the tile floor.

"That's quite a goose egg you've got there, Mr. Nelson," the young nurse said.

He sat up in the chair they'd placed him in and winced from the headache.

"What happened?"

"Apparently you were overcome again with your son's condition, sir. Now don't feel embarrassed. I've seen this happen so many times before, I couldn't count them."

"You're very kind," he said and slumped back down into the worn vinyl chair.

"Well, keep that ice on it for awhile—it'll help with the swelling. I'll check back in on you two later."

After receiving her wake-up call at 7 a.m., Monika Nelson showered and stood in front of the oversized bathroom mirror to brush her hair. Why did they have to put such huge mirrors in these hotels? She removed the towel that she'd wrapped herself in and looked at it again. It was always there. The horrible, disfiguring scar that had made her feel so repulsive that she still couldn't make love with Michael, even though it had been a whole year since her mastectomy. She didn't feel like a whole woman anymore. She hated the prosthetic breast. She hated cancer for stealing her attractiveness from her.

Oh God. Poor Rodney—imagine the painful scarring he'll have from the burns. And he was so handsome! How will he take it? The girls always swarmed around him in high school—now he'll likely be shunned and stared at. That's okay. I'm his mother and I'll care for him. He can move back in with us and we'll be a family again, and he'll never have to be alone. We'll shield him from the rude stares and cruelty. We can do this.

****

Back at the hospital, Michael Nelson was startled by alarms going off on the monitors attached to his son. Within seconds, the nurses and orderlies were checking the readouts in horror. "Call Dr. Aiken STAT!" "Call a code!" Rod's heart had stopped.

"Get me some epinephrine! Draw a blood gas now!" The code blue drew staff from all over the hospital, emergency room supervisors and doctors. There was a frenzy of activity and orders flying. "What—why isn't the crash cart in here? For God's sake, somebody get the crash cart." A Nursing Supervisor flew past Mike and pushed him out in the hall as she went to wheel the small cart with the defibrillator on it into the room. The paddles were lubricated and the doctor cried out, "Clear" and Rod's body raised off the bed from the current of electricity flowing from the machine to shock his heart. Everyone held their breath and looked at the monitor. "Okay, people—turn it up to thirty. Clear!" Again, Rod's body convulsed with the jolt of electricity. Everyone looked at the monitor again, and sighed with relief as the flat line on the EKG machine became the uneven, jagged up and down pattern of a normal heartbeat again.

Dr. Aiken put the defibrillator paddles back on the cart and walked out to talk with Michael in the hall. "Mr. Nelson, that was close. It confounds me how a patient can seem to be improving and suddenly take a drastic turn for the worst like that. He's not out of the woods yet. This proves it."

Mike was ashen and shaking. "What can you do to make sure this doesn't happen again?"

The doctor shook his head, looked back at his patient and shrugged his shoulders. "We're already doing everything we can. We've drawn some blood for tests that might tell us more about why it happened, but the most we can do is more of the same. I wish I had more details for you. I'll see you this evening."

Staff was still streaming out of Rod's room as Monika hurried to the door. "Michael—Rod—what's happened? Why didn't you call me?" Her husband tried to pull her near him but again she pushed him aside.

"Honey, Rod's heart stopped. But they got it going again."

She had fire in her eyes. "Damn you, Mike. You didn't call me? I told you—"

"Monny, it just happened. Just now. There was no time to call you. It was over as quickly as it began. Honey, you know—"

"I don't care what you say. Our son was dying and you made no attempt to call me. I'll never forgive you for this! Never!" She shoved him out of her way and pushed her way past the nurses to her son's side. And that's where she stayed for the next 24 hours.

****

The two women were silent as they motored along Route 264 from Virginia Beach to the airport. Mary's thoughts were already in San

Diego, eager to be there searching the wards in the naval hospital for Jimmy. Margie was searching for the right words to convince her daughter not to go. The radio played "Happy Together," by the Turtles as Margie lit a cigarette, took a long drag and shifted nervously in her seat.

"Mary, you're a grown, married woman. I know you got shafted when you got me for a ma, and you haven't gotten a hell of a lot of motherly advice from me before, but I hate to see you goin' clear out there to California all alone and going to see all those poor souls in the hospital, only to be disappointed again. I could see it if there was some chance of him bein' there, but…"

Mary smiled but didn't take her eyes off the road. "Mom, I think there is a chance. I think there's a real good chance. Military hospitals are full of men from the Forrestal, some of them so bandaged up that you can hardly see an eye on their face. Come on, you know I have to go. I can't stop looking for him until I'm sure. You saw the letter yourself—they don't even know if we buried the right man, for God's sake."

Margie took a long, slow draw on her smoke and fought back tears. Damned cryin', she thought. She never got so emotional until after she quit drinking. A red out-of-state Chevelle Malibu flashed past their car and it cut back in front of them. Crazy damned kids, Margie thought, driving like maniacs these days. They don't have any notion how fragile life is. They think they're immortal. Don't know nothin' about life yet. Poor Mary—life dealt her a rotten hand to start out with and now look where she is. Goin' 2700 miles across the country to look for a dead husband. Jeeze, a drink would be good right now, she thought.

Mary pulled her mustang up to the curb outside the American Airlines terminal. "You gonna be okay?" she said.

"Me? Heck, it's not me I'm worryin' about—you know that. Are you sure you're gonna be okay?

Mary reached across and patted her mother's leg. "Come on, Mom, you know I'm gonna be all right. I'll call you as soon as I check into the hotel and like I said, if he's not there, I'll be back in a couple of days." Leaning across the seat, she kissed her mom on the forehead. "Now don't you worry!" Both women smiled, each thinking about how much closer they were now than a few months ago.

A cabbie was blowing his horn, so Mary got out and took her suitcase out of the backseat. "Take care, Mom. I love ya." Margie scooted over to the driver's side and pretended to adjust the mirrors as she watched her daughter walk away. A little surprised by the outfit Mary chose for the day, a white and blue striped sleeveless top and a white miniskirt and tall soft white glove leather boots. I sure as heck hope they don't start makin' those skirts any shorter, she thought. She turned around and scowled at the cab driver when he gave her another toot on his horn.

Ticket and boarding pass for seat number 16A in hand, Mary stepped into the passenger compartment of the plane and smiled back at the airline attendant. Good, she thought, a window seat. It was her first time aboard a plane and she was hoping that she'd be able to see everything clearly, but she had first-time jitters too. Heck, it was only her second time out of Virginia, she thought, as she watched a man stow his briefcase in the overhead compartment. She buckled up and looked out the small window at the flurry of activity by the airline crew, still driving in with luggage carts.

More and more passengers continued filling the aircraft, but no one came to claim the seat next to Mary yet. Good, she thought. Maybe no one'll be there to witness her white knuckles during takeoff. That and the landing were the only two parts of the flight that had her nervous. And it took a lot to make Mary Gallant nervous. She could hear the jet engines screaming as they were awakened, and it seemed the whole fuselage shuddered from their fury at being forced from their slumber.

"'Scuse me, this is 18B, right?" a voice asked.

"Yes." Mary turned away from the window. "Oh my gosh. Doctor Boyer?"

"What do you suppose the chances of this happening in a lifetime are?" he grinned and stashed his attache in the overhead compartment. "How have you been, Mary? You still never called for an appointment."

"I'm fine, thanks. I can't believe… "I've been meaning to call—oh, I have to warn you about something. This is my first flight. Where do

THEY NEVER REALLY LEAVE

they keep those little bags on here?" He laughed and pointed at the pouch in the back of the seat ahead of hers.

"I'm sure you won't need it. You're a tough cookie, after what I've seen you come out of. You going to San Diego too?" Mary nodded. Within sixteen minutes the plane was finally taxiing toward a runway. The takeoff was incredible to Mary, the engines roaring as the plane sped down the strip. As the nose of the plane left the ground and the aircraft tilted sharply toward the sky Mary gasped and her hand innocently found Doctor Mike's arm for security.

She withdrew her hand quickly. "Oh, I'm sorry. It's just that I didn't expect—I didn't know what to expect, I guess."

"That's okay," he smiled. "See, you didn't even need the paper bag!" The plane's ascent became more level and Mary looked out the tiny window at the shrinking world below. "So, what's taking you to San Diego?" The one question she was hoping he wouldn't ask. She suddenly felt an adrenaline rush and became very defensive. All she needed right now was one more person to try to convince her how hopeless her mission was. They'd really given her the business at work, and her mother's comments didn't do much to encourage her. Now her doctor was going to no doubt go on about the efficiency of the military and how mistakes like this just don't happen in this day and age.

All she needed was one more naysayer. One more negative voice, and she felt like she'd fall apart. But as Dr. Boyer listened, she went into detail about Jimmy's reported death and the funeral and then the confusing letter the Navy sent her. She braced herself for the regular reaction, but he surprised her. He said with all the furor and confusion that must've been going on aboard that ship, wasn't anything possible? And with explosions going off and fires, the injuries those poor men were receiving could certainly mask or at least muddy their identity. She sunk back in her seat like a deflated balloon—relieved that someone else saw hope too. Her eyes actually sparkled for the first time in months. Someone else believed Jimmy could be alive!

"In fact, Mary, I may be able to help you. I'm going to that same military hospital to check out a new surgical procedure the Navy is pioneering. Maybe I could talk to someone and open some doors for you."

"Really?" She peered into his eyes. "They gave me a really hard time at Portsmouth. That would be wonderful if you could help me." She knew it wasn't a mistake to go to San Diego. "How can I ever thank you, Doc?"

"Well, you could have dinner with me before you leave town."

She felt as though he'd plunged a dagger into her gut. Her face felt hot, turned red and angry tears welled up in her eyes. "I'll tell you what, Doctor Boyer, you can forget about dinner. In fact, I don't need or want your help at the hospital, either. You really have a hell of a lot of nerve. Hitting on a girl who's just lost her husband. Or maybe just not lost her husband. Whatever the case, I think you're crummy." The seatbelt light went off and she pushed past him to head back to the ladies' room.

When she returned to her seat a few minutes later, the doctor stood to let her by. "Mary, I'm so sorry. Sometimes my mouth engages before my brain stops it. I didn't mean to come on to you, or offend you. I just had in mind a casual meal between two out-of-towners. I learned a lot when I was treating you back in Virginia."

"Like what?"

He lowered his voice. "Like how much will a person can have to live. That maniac raped you, he demoralized you, stabbed and tortured you, took your child from you, and left you in a ditch to die; but you still had the tenacity to fight for your life. I've seen so many people give up under much less serious circumstances. You're going thousands of miles all alone to search for him. He's a lucky man."

"Thanks, Doc. But let's drop the dinner stuff, okay?"

"Okay, Mary. Sorry I brought it up." She leaned toward the window to pretend to drift off to sleep; the doctor turned the page of the magazine he was pretending to read and tried not to think about her long, sexy legs that had slipped past him earlier.

"Something to drink, sir?" Mary stirred and sat up as she heard the doctor's answer.

"Yes, I'll have a ginger ale, please."

THEY NEVER REALLY LEAVE

"There you go, sir, ma'm?"

"Coffee. Black, thank you."

"Did you have a nice nap?" He smiled broadly, showing his perfect white teeth.

"Uh, yeah; I guess I needed it." She looked at her watch. "Jeeze, it's noon. We've been back up in the air another hour and a half already. I'm glad we didn't have to change planes in Atlanta. The airport back home was bad enough. I hate to think what San Diego's going to be like."

"I'm sure you'll be fine. Hey, just look at the beautiful blue sky out there, isn't it something?"

Mary leaned closer to her window.

"Yeah, the clouds are all below us, like big tufts of cotton. It's beautiful." Mary averted her eyes away from the young doctor's handsome face and back out the airplane window.

He replied, "Yes, it sure is."

"I never knew what it was like to climb above the clouds. It's kinda spooky up here though, like we're all alone and no one else exists. Like there isn't even an earth down there," she said.

The doctor grinned again. "Yeah, you know, I can remember thinking that the first time I flew, too. It's like a whole different world up here."

The small talk came a little easier now and they chatted about Doctor Boyer's family and his hometown back in Ohio. Mary told him a few stories about her mom and they both laughed, especially about the baseball bat and Jimmy.

"I had a feeling she was feisty the day I walked into your hospital room, before she even said a word," he joked. He took the last sip of his ginger ale and leaned back in his seat, stretching his back. "Mary, would you reconsider my dinner invitation? Here," he pulled a pad from his pocket and wrote down his hotel name and room number for her. "If you do change your mind, here's where I'll be staying. And I'll see the Medical Director at the hospital, I'm sure we can open some doors for you and make it easier, whether or not we have dinner, okay?"

She took the note, hesitantly. "Okay, I'll take this. But don't plan on me changing my mind, Doc. Not that I don't appreciate it." She thought for a moment, then said "I didn't bring anything fancy to wear, anyway."

"Oh, that wouldn't be a problem," he said. "We could easily find somewhere casual-there are hundreds of restaurants in San Diego near the hospital."

"Well, don't hold your breath, okay? No offense." She fiddled with her seatbelt and looked out her window again at the billowing clouds below them. "Just—well, I'll see. I guess we have about 3 1/2 hours left before we get to California."

It was an incredible first time flying for Mary, but she couldn't help thinking that it would've been a lot easier to enjoy it if handsome Doctor Boyer hadn't been seated beside her all the way. Hours later when the plane finally touched down in San Diego, she was already gearing herself up for the task ahead of her.

After collecting her luggage she caught a taxi outside the terminal. The local Ho-Jo's where she had reservations was about twenty minutes away, but it was near the hospital. She checked in and hurried to her room with her two small suitcases. Closing the door behind her, she dropped her bags and sprang upon the bed, exhausted, and dozed off. When she woke up, the clock on the bedside stand said it was 2:45 p.m. Mary sat up, rubbed her eyes and stretched. She looked around the neat, clean little room and walked over to the window to pull open the heavy green drapes. Outside in the California sunshine, palm trees arched over a congested freeway and to the right of her view stood the San Diego Navy Hospital. The clean white brick facade made even the exterior of the building look sterile and cold. Was he in there, somewhere? He has to be. Hold on, Jimmy, I'm coming to you, baby. Just hold on.

She turned from the window and sat down on the bed to call her mom. "Hello, Mom? It's me. Yeah, I'm here, I made it. The flight was okay, really kinda neat. I'll tell you all about that when I get back. I just wanted to let you know that I'm here. Huh? No, it's only about ten to three here, I'm three hours behind you now, remember. I dozed off on my bed here after I checked into the hotel for awhile. Yeah, I'm going to go to the dining room downstairs to get something to eat. No, everything's fine Mom, I'm just tired from the flight. I'll call you tomorrow sometime. Love you too, bye." Mary thought, there was no way she was about to tell her mother that she was sitting next to Doctor Boyer all during the eight and a half hour flight. After she thought about it for a minute, she wondered why she shouldn't have.

The next day was a daunting replay of Mary's experience in Portsmouth Naval Hospital, the only bright point being that Doctor Boyer had made good on his promise to open some doors for her. At least she didn't have to fight her way in again. The nursing staff was polite and very understanding, but bed after bed the young woman again had to face burned and mutilated men, looking back at her with eyes full of desperation and pain that begged for an end to their suffering. If it wasn't enough that she'd traveled over 3,000 miles across the country for nothing, now she had to go home knowing that all hope was gone for ever finding Jimmy alive.

Her life was over. She couldn't go back to the life she had before Jimmy, she just couldn't. She wouldn't. To have finally been so happy, so complete and then to have that ripped away from you… God, it wasn't fair! He was her one chance, her only chance for happiness. There would never be another love for her. Back in her hotel room, Mary sat on the edge of her bed and sobbed. For the first time in weeks, she really cried with all her might, releasing all of her pent-up disappointment and frustration. She clawed at the bedding and pulled it from the bed, tossing it violently across the room in a heap. Clinging to her pillow, she fell back on the bare mattress and curled up.

Jimmy, oh Jimmy! Why did I ever let you go? I should have done something. I should have talked you into going awol. My Jimmy! How could I have been so stupid? I knew something was wrong even before you ever left the port…

Her temples were pounding as the phone rang. She let it ring for several minutes, then feared it might be her mother and answered it.

"Hello?"

"Hi, is this Mary? Mary Gallant?"

"Yes, who's this?"

"This is Doctor Boyer, Mary. Mary, have you been crying?"

"Uh, yeah, I have been. No luck at the hospital today, but thank you for your help Doc. Listen, no offense, but I had a real bad day and—"

"You're sure you won't change your mind about dinner? It may help a little to get out of your room for a while."

Mary pulled a lock of her long, shiny red hair back behind her ear and snifled. "No, I can't make it. I've got a really rotten headache and I'm going to make some calls and see if I can catch an earlier flight back home. But thank you. Thanks a lot." She didn't wait for his response, but returned the receiver to the cradle and reached for the box of tissues. She felt guilty and stupid for having even considered having dinner with her doctor. She picked up the phone and dialed her mom's number.

"Hi, Mom?" She no sooner got the words out than she fell apart again, weeping uncontrollably. Her mother knew what Mary was about to tell her. In fact, she had something even worse to tell her daughter.

After she listened to Mary's story for a few minutes, Margie started. "Mary, they took him."

"What?"

"They went out to the damned cemetery and dug him up and took him!"

"Oh my God, why? Who took him?"

"You know, the military. The Navy. They came and took him and wouldn't tell me nothin' when I called."

"Why those sonofa…" Mary's tears of sorrow turned into searing rage. "When?"

"Today. Just today they done it. I tried to call the cops and see if they could do anything, but they gave me the runaround too."

"Damn! Damn them all! Mom, I'll be home as soon as I can. I don't want you talking to anyone or letting anyone in your house or mine, understand? Who the hell do they think they are? I'm hanging up and calling the airport to get the next flight back home. I don't care if I have to be up all night, I'll be there as soon as I can, Mom. She slammed the phone down and stuffed her face into the pillow to stifle her scream.

Chapter 14

"Mary—" Margie's hand covered her mouth. She was shocked by her daughter's disheveled appearance. Mary always took pride in keeping herself looking nice. But the girl arriving in the airport that day, in a wrinkled pale pink nehru jacket and jeans, no makeup, her hair tousled and unkempt barely looked like her daughter. The other passengers from flight 205 were crowding past the two women to meet with their own relatives or friends.

"I know, mother, I look like crap. I feel like crap too. Let's just get my bags and get outta here," Mary said as she pushed her mother on ahead of her toward the baggage claim area.

Mary pulled the car into the short driveway beside her apartment. Margie asked, "You want me to stick around for a little while, honey? In case you wanna talk?"

"Yeah, that would be okay. Thanks, mom." Once inside, they made a pot of coffee and sat down at the kitchen table. Both fidgety, they sipped from their cups and were silent for a long time. The apartment was stale and muggy from the hot summer day. Margie wiped her brow with the back of her hand and lit a cigarette. She wished that she had the right words to comfort her daughter. She searched and searched within herself for something, anything that would make Mary feel better. When words did come, they seemed hollow and inadequate.

"Mary, I just wanna say that I love you. I can still remember how much it hurts to think that you've found the man you've been waiting for all your life and then lose him. I'm an old woman now, but I'll always remember waiting at the dock for my sailor to come back to me. Now I know that I became a bitter old drunk after that happened, and I just don't want to see that happen to you. I'm only sayin' this because I care about you, you know."

Mary didn't reply, but she stood and walked over to the large picture window overlooking the beach. Cradling her cup of coffee close to her in her left hand, she gestured with her right, sweeping motions across the water. "Look at the sea, mother. No one on earth can stop it from its course. No one can contain it, or stop it, or release it. It ebbs and flows at its own will. You could go down there and stomp and scream until you were hoarse, and it wouldn't stop for you." She held her free hand over her heart. "I know he's out there. Alive. I do. I tried to believe that he's dead, but my heart won't let me. My head was trying to make my heart believe it, but when you have a love like mine and Jimmy's, no matter how far away your love goes, they never really leave. And my heart knows that he's out there, waiting for me to find him. I have to keep looking. I can't give up on him. I can't, mom. He's as much alive as you and I are."

Margie smiled. "Ah, my Mary. Always the strong one. But where are you gonna look now?" Mary just shook her head. He mother ground out the cigarette she was smoking and walked over to the window beside her daughter, putting her arm around her waist. "You still amaze me, kiddo."

"Well, I don't feel very amazing, mom, I feel like a big zero." She had a far away look on her face. "Jimmy's out there somewhere, hurt who knows how badly, waiting for me and I can't find him." She placed a palm against her belly, where their unborn child was once, but was no more. "And the damned Navy sure isn't being any great help to me. Why, mom? It's so wrong." She leaned against the windowpane. "Why would they send me that weird letter and go out to the cemetery to exhume the body if they were sure it was him?"

Margie nodded and shrugged her shoulders. "The bastards. They know they screwed up and they just aren't tellin' anybody nothin' until they can fix it or cover it up."

Mary smiled as she turned toward her, hands on her hips. "So now you're starting to believe me? Well, I could rot sitting here waiting for them to figure it out and level with me, as if they ever would." She picked up her jacket, keys and purse. I'm going over to the base right now."

"And what do ya think you're gonna find over there? They wouldn't tell me nothin' the other day. I think you should get some rest."

"I don't know what I'll find, mom. But I'm gonna knock on every door I can find until I get someone to listen to me. I'll see you later— you might as well go home. Thanks for sitting with me for a while."

Chaplain Byerly ushered Mary into his office and motioned for her to sit in a chair on the other side of his very organized, well-polished heavy walnut desk. He was a frail old guy, with a shiny dome of a scalp and only the hint of a crown of short white hair around it. He fidgeted nervously with his hands, wringing them and clearing his voice each time he spoke, and avoided making eye contact whenever possible. He had eyeglasses that were thick as a Coke bottle but he listened carefully as Mary told him the story of how Jimmy was first listed as missing, then dead, and the mysterious letter that she'd gotten about a mix-up.

"And now I find out that whoever it was that I buried as my husband has been dug back up by the Navy and they won't tell my family anything about it!" She leaned across his shiny, neat desk and glared, "With all due respect, chaplain, can you help me find out what the hell is going on?"

The elderly man smiled nervously and adjusted one of the pictures that faced him on his desk. His eyes grew big as saucers and he was mortified by a smudge that she'd left when she leaned across his prized walnut desk. "Well, Mrs. Gallant—"

"Please, call me Mary."

He cleared his throat. "Well, Mary, the Forrestal incident was a terrible, terrible tragedy and an awful blow to the fleet. Just terrible. I've personally dealt with nearly a third of the families who lost loved ones in the accident. From what I've been told, the Navy goes through very painstaking steps to verify identification of the injured and dead."

"Well, one of their painstaking steps screwed up! Haven't you been listening to me? They don't know where my husband really is! They let me grieve over him and bury him and now they've gone and reclaimed his body for reasons they refuse to give!" Mary stood to her feet, towering over the frail old guy. "Now, can you help me or not? I don't have time to waste if you're just going to give me some damned runaround, I've got to find him! I swear, if someone doesn't level with me soon, I'm gonna go nuts!"

Captain Byerly reached to straighten the same picture on his desk again, scratching behind an ear. He cleared his throat. "Uh, Mary," He motioned for her to sit back down. "I want to try and help you, I just don't know—"

"Same old sh—"

"Mary, I said I want to try and help you, now please sit down and let me think. This is highly irregular—I've never come across anything like it."

Mary sat down and crossed her legs, smoothing her skirt and scooting her chair closer to his desk. "You're tellin' me? How do you think I feel?"

"Yes, hmm…" He flipped through his rolodex and peered down through his bifocals at a phone number. "This is really rather awkward, but all I can think to do is to try getting in touch with the Base Commander and see if he's available to come over here right now to meet with us."

Mary smacked a hand down on his desk with glee, leaving a smudge that alarmed him, but said, "Now you're talkin' Chaplain! Go to it, man!"

"Now Mary, I can't guarantee that he's willing even if he's in his office right now. He's a busy man." He smiled, looking hopeful. "But we'll just have a go at it, okay?"

"Right—I mean, thank you, Chaplain." Her heart was ready to explode out of her chest as he dialed the number.

"Hello—yes, this is Captain Byerly calling for Admiral Rivero. No, he's not expecting my call. Yes, I'll wait." He scratched his nose, frowned at the smudge on his polished desk and adjusted his thick glasses.

"Uh, yes, Admiral Rivero? This is Mason Byerly. Thanks for taking my call, sir. Yes, I'm doing just fine. Uh-huh." He pulled at his collar and leaned back in his chair. "Well, Admiral, the reason I'm calling you is that I have a real situation over here in my office. The wife of one of the poor souls on the Forrestal is in here and you won't believe the story she's just told me. Yes, I realize that, sir. Well, this is something that hasn't come up before, at least to my knowledge. I know how busy you are sir, but I was hoping that you could give us an hour of your time to come over and hear her story. She's very distraught, and I believe she needs someone higher up the chain of command to assist her." He laughed nervously, and cleared his throat. "Yes, sir, so I went all the way to the top, to you. You can? Oh, that's fine, sir, that's real fine. We'll be waiting. Thank you, sir. Goodbye."

The shaken man looked at Mary, gave a heavy sigh and regrouped for a moment. He walked over to the coffee pot in the corner of his office and poured two cups. "He'll be here in an hour. Meanwhile, why don't you tell me again what that letter said."

"Tell you, I can show you. I have everything right here—"

"Why doesn't that surprise me?" he said as he grinned and he handed her a cup.

Mary reached into a large folder that she'd brought in with her containing the strange letter, the official military death certificate and posthumous medals that were awarded Jimmy, and his dental records. She took the cup of coffee from the chaplain and pushed the stack of papers across the desk for him to inspect.

"Well, Mrs. Gallant, uh, Mary, if what you say is true, I would venture to say that a major investigation will have to be launched over this, and believe me, the Navy will not take this travesty lightly."

"Chaplain Byerly, what I say is true. And I know that my husband is out there somewhere. Alive. When I visited the hospitals, I walked past scores of men who were bandaged up so tightly that I wouldn't have known him if I walked right past him. He's alive! I know he is." The two talked on about Jimmy and the events leading up to now until a knock came at the office door. The chaplain opened it to find the Admiral standing there, good to his word, exactly one hour from when he'd called him.

The Admiral was a handsome, middle-aged Hispanic man, seemed young to be a full Admiral, Mary thought. "Ah, Mason. Good to see you. Haven't seen you around the officer's club for a few days, you all right?"

"Yes sir, I've got a bit of a cold, but nothing to be concerned about. Let me introduce you to Mrs. Mary Gallant. She's the wife of Petty Officer James Gallant."

"Nice to meet you, my condolences in the loss of your husband m'am—"

"He's not lost, the Navy just can't find him," Mary said abruptly. He's alive, that's what this is all about." The Admiral looked at her quizzically.

"Tell me everything, Mrs. Gallant; from the beginning. You have my undivided attention.

Unlike the chaplain, the Admiral was composed and mildly detached as he listened to Mary's chilling tale. When she was finished, he stood and faced them both.

"Well, Mrs. Gallant, it's a fantastic story. Given the dedication and professionalism of our medical staffs in our land-based hospitals and aboard our ships, it's difficult to believe that such a mistake could be made. Very difficult." Mary held her breath. "But have Chaplain Byerly photocopy everything that you have there and give him your address and phone number. Mason, send it all over to my office marked "Confidential" to my attention. I'll have my personal assistant get started on it by the first of the week."

Mary leapt to her feet, "Oh, thank you, Admiral. Thank God. I didn't think I was ever going to get someone to listen to me."

"You're welcome, m'am. I can't guarantee what we'll find, but we will get to the bottom of this for you. Mason," he nodded and was out the door.

Mary was so excited that she hugged the frail old chaplain. "Thank you, chaplain. Thank you so much." He smiled sweetly, a little embarrassed by the hug from such a beautiful young woman.

That night, Mary lay awake, her window open, listening to the tide wash over the shore. Each time another wave swept over the soft sand where earth met sea, it shushed softly. It sounded so much like the way Jimmy would shush her when she'd try to talk when they were making love. Shhhh… he would say, and pull her close to him, lavishing his kisses on her neck and shoulders. How she longed to feel him next to her once more. Shhhh… the sea whispered to her. Tomorrow, she would return to work for the first time in five weeks. How was she going to answer the prodding questions now, and deal with the patronizing stares? How was she going to put up a good front, and appear to be the same old tough, stoic Mary? And how was she going to endure the jerks that she was going to have to serve? Shhhh… again replied the sea as she drifted off to sleep.

Chapter 15

The next day at the Chesapeake Crab house was far easier on Mary than she'd thought it would be. Well into September now, the tourist season had ebbed once more as it did every year. Sandy kept her myriad of inept questions and probing to herself. Chet took her aside a few times just to ask her how she was holding up and if there was anything he could do.

She raced home in her Mustang to phone her mother and see if anyone had called. Just in case, she'd given her work number and her mother's phone number with Chaplain Byerly. There was no word yet. Why would there be? It was the military. Mary slid a t.v. dinner into the oven and turned on the television.

Not much on, except more footage of the continued assaults on the North Vietnamese and how many more of our soldiers were being lost. She watched it and listened to Walter Cronkite until the buzzer went off on the kitchen stove, then she walked over and flicked the television off.

Somewhere between the re-cooked green beans and the apple cobbler of the t.v. dinner, she decided to visit the Portsmouth Naval

THEY NEVER REALLY LEAVE

Hospital again that evening. It was, after all, such a short distance away. She hadn't made a very good impression the first time she was there, so Mary cautioned herself to try and be polite and patient. After finishing her meal, she changed her clothes and headed toward Portsmouth.

Lt. Kipfer wasn't on duty that day. A much more congenial Ltcdr Bryant was, and though she was astonished by Mary's story she was willing to let her into the wards to walk among the wounded again. From the time she walked through the open doors, the putrid smell of decaying and regenerating flesh stung Mary's nostrils as it had before, and many of the same bandaged, pain-racked men remained; tearful eyes staring out at her from behind yards of bandages and antibiotic ointment.

Most of the men lay in their hospital beds all alone, no family or friends there to hold their hands or comfort them. Mary's heart ached to see all those poor troops so badly burned and in agony, with no one by their sides. There were a few wives and mothers present, who tried to dote over their loved one and straighten bedcovers and fluff pillows, whatever they could do. Mary was consumed with despair to be beside Jimmy, fluffing his pillow or just sitting quietly next to his side.

One woman stood out from among the rest. She was dressed very properly, in an ivy green-checkered jacket dress with four black buttons across the top. She sat up erect in a chair next to a bed that held her bandage-swathed loved one. She eyed Mary as she crossed in front of her, sniffed her disapproval, then returned her gaze to the one in the bed. Mary paused just long enough to read the name on the foot of the bed. ABM2 Rodney Nelson.

As she moved on to the next bed, she found a sad fellow sitting up in his bed with fresh skin grafts gleaming across his cheeks and nose, and the rest of his face covered. He was softly sobbing, reaching out to her with his bandaged, stump hands. No one sat beside this one, either. AMM2 Sam Higley. Mary thought about it for a minute, then took a seat by his bed, talking softly to him, trying to comfort him. She was afraid to touch him; she knew from a little reading she'd done that infection is the greatest enemy of skin grafts. She only whispered to him, "Shhh, it's gonna be all right. You've got good people here taking care of you, and you're gonna pull through this. Just keep fighting." Keep fighting. Who was she to tell him to keep fighting? Monika Nelson didn't like this local yokel snooping around so near to her son. "Who does she think she is?" She asked herself. She turned around and glared, as if Mary was disturbing her.

Sam Higley lay perfectly still, a tube going down his throat to breathe for him. The machine next to his bed inhaled and exhaled for him, sending fresh air into his lungs. Another small red rubber tube, clamped off at the end, ran up his nose. Mary crossed her legs and kicked something soft that hung beside the bed. She pulled back the cover slightly to see that it was a bag full of amber-colored urine. She pointed it out to a busy corpsman who left and returned with a large metal measuring can to empty it. When she stood to leave, Sam Higley's eyes filled with tears. She promised him that she'd stop back by again the next time she was in the hospital.

The well-dressed woman who glared contemptuously at her intrigued Mary. ABM2 Rodney Nelson. Was it her husband or her son? Monika guarded her boy like a mother hen. No, more like a mother bear. Mary couldn't even get close enough to her to ask her a few questions, like she could the other visitors that day. Most people were tired but happy to tell how heroic their loved one was and how strongly he or she was fighting to make it. But still no Jimmy. After 2 1/2 hours on the burns wards, Mary left for home.

Walking barefoot along the beach that evening, she felt for the first time as though every drop of hope had been drained from her body. The sun was setting in the east and the water had taken on its dark evening hue. She left small footprints in the soft, wet sand, and the water had the chill of a September evening low tide.

"Oh God, it's not fair," she thought. "I can feel myself buckling under the possibility that maybe Jimmy wasn't ever going to be found alive. But I can't give up on him! Jimmy was everything I'd every dreamed of in a man."

She remembered that first night that they met, when he knocked the candle onto the wooden deck floor and panicked the other customers. She laughed out loud, remembering him sitting there, balancing that stupid table on three legs, trying to act cool when he'd just done one of the most un-cool things she'd ever seen. And the look on his face when he found out that she was the manager of the joint!

On down the shore she ambled, past nightfall, just re-living the short time that they had together. She thought about how mad she was when he showed up at her house and refused to leave until she agreed to go out with him. She laughed and shook her head remembering him catching her at the Super Shopper and seeing how banged up he was from her mom's baseball bat. She thought about the night they were married, and the hotel room with all the roses. She could almost feel his tender touch as they made love for the first time, afterward coiled up in bed together, her head against his smooth, strong chest. She recalled meeting his parents for the first time and how nervous she was, but then how welcome they made her feel when they arrived.

God! This was too much to lose! How did God expect her to go on without Jimmy? The ocean had turned gloomy and ominous after dark, and she turned to head back toward home, not realizing that she'd walked a whole five miles down the shoreline.

After Mary made her way back to her empty, lonely apartment, she poured a cup of milk and sat down on the davenport, flicking on the small radio on the end stand. She searched around the dial, trying to find a station that was not playing love songs or sad Country ballads. There was something about that unfriendly woman at the hospital that bothered her, and she didn't even know what it was. Something that didn't add up. Why would a stranger be so guarded and suspicious? Even if she was just an overprotective mother who was distraught over her son's dire condition, why would she react to people that way? Mary felt sorry for her and was mad at her at the same time. She just couldn't get her out of her mind, maybe that's was all it was. She pissed her off. She made her feel attacked, judged for no earthly reason. You could always tell someone with money, Mary thought. She finished her milk, stretched out on the couch and fell asleep.

The next morning, Mary was awakened by the phone ringing. Disoriented and clumsy, she fumbled to the kitchen to answer it. "Hello?"

"Hi honey, it's mom. How's it goin'?"

Mary leaned against the wall and reached up with a hand to fluff her tousled, unbrushed scarlet hair. "Oh, okay. What time is it? Ten a.m. already? Wow—I fell asleep on the couch. You just woke me up."

"Oh, sorry—"

"—No, that's okay. I needed to get up anyways. Good thing I'm not working the morning shift today! How are you, mom?"

"Doin' fine, hon. But I did just get a call—"

"—You did? From the Navy?"

"Yup." Mary was suddenly fully awake.

"Well, what did they say? Mom?"

"Ah, they didn't say nothin', honey. Same as always, just that they were still working on it. Some Lieutenant Commander McGee said he was working on it, left his phone number for you."

Mary grabbed a pencil. "What is it?" She demanded. "Okay, I got it. Yeah, I'll call him right now. Thanks a lot, mom. No, I can't meet you for lunch today. I don't know if I'll be meeting with them again or not before I go in to work today. Thanks for the offer, anyway. Bye."

She dialed feverishly and a secretary answered. "I'm calling for Lieutenant Commander McGee? This is Mary Gallant, he called and left his number for me. Yes, I'll hold on." She was soaring into high gear now. A whole pot of coffee wouldn't have stimulated her anymore than this news. "What do you mean he's not in? He just called this morning." She listened as the secretary explained that he was on the base but not in his office. "Well, please tell him to call me at my house, 455-0909, not my mother's. I'll be here all day until 3 p.m. this afternoon. After then he can call me at work. Yes, he has that number too. Thank you." With a crack, she slammed the phone back on its cradle. "Damn!"

Mary held vigil by her telephone all day, up to the very minute that she had to dress and leave for work. There was no return call, and still none during her shift. She spent a restless night's sleep that night, still thinking about Jimmy, still thinking about the odd woman in the hospital, still fuming that the Admiral's assistant hadn't called her back yet.

She awoke Wednesday morning to the sound of the waves crashing and the seagulls screeching outside. Since she didn't have to work until the dinner shift, she decided to hurry over to the Portsmouth Naval Hospital again and take another look. Maybe somebody's bandages would have been removed by now, maybe a patient would have been transferred in. Maybe that goofy, unfriendly woman would be around again.

When Mary went into the ward that day, there were a couple of men who had some bandages and she was able to walk up to them and get a better look. Each time, she'd pause and try to smile at their puffy, red bloated faces covered in ointment and gave a word or two of encouragement before moving on. Even if one of them was Jimmy, it would be nearly impossible to tell, because of the severity of their burns. Many were still hooked up to breathing tubes so they couldn't speak to her, and their arms were immobilized also. Would she ever be able to speak to them?

The rude woman was absent that morning. There was a gray-haired man sleeping in the chair that she'd occupied the day before. He wore a shirt with a dark tie, a gray wool cardigan and black slacks. He had a fancy tweed coat thrown over his lap. He had to have been there all night, he was snoring up a storm. Mary edged over to the foot of the bed and smoothed her hand over the name and rank that was listed for the patient. "ABM2 Rodney Nelson," she whispered. Bandages covered every inch of him, it seemed; and tubes were coming out from his nose and mouth. The black bellow inside the respirator next to his bed filled and emptied as it breathed for him.

She moved cautiously to the other side of the bed and stood there over him. If the man in the chair awoke, would he be as snobbish and unfriendly as the woman had been? She could hardly breathe. Suddenly the patient in the bed opened his eyes and looked directly at Mary. It was him! She knew it from the moment she looked into his beautiful blue eyes again. She jarred the bed a bit as she grabbed on to its rails to keep from collapsing as his eyes became puddles of tears… She reached over the bed rails and gently caressed the bandaged face that looked up at her. "Jimmy!" "Oh, Jimmy," she whispered. Mary's own tears spotted the bed linen below as she leaned toward him; she was shaking all over, and her beautiful, wavy scarlet hair hung across Jimmy's chest once more.

"What the hell do you think you're doing? Get away from my son!" The woman lunged at Mary, knocking her away from the bed. "Get away, who do you think you are?"

"You crazy woman, get away from me!" Mary shoved the crazed woman and sent her tumbling to the floor.

"Monika, what are you doing?" Mike Nelson stirred in his chair.

She said nothing, but was determined to get the stranger away from her son. She pounced again, one hand going around Mary's slender throat and the other grabbing a handful of her long red hair. "Take your hands off of my son! Michael, damn you, do something! Call a nurse!" Mary choked and coughed as the woman's stranglehold dug her nails into her throat. She tried to push the crazed woman away again, but instead elbowed her hard in the gut, knocking the wind out of Monika Nelson. When she went down, the older woman took two i.v. poles with her, disconnecting both the clear fluid and the nasal tube from Jimmy. She scrambled to her feet again and pinned Mary to the wall, this time disconnecting the ventilator tubes. Alarms began to go off as the machine stopped breathing for the patient.

Mary pushed against Monika, but she had her out-weighed by at least thirty pounds. "You crazy bitch! Now look what you've done," Mary said. "Oh my God, the ventilator!" She ordered to Mike Nelson, "Go get the nurse, now—move it—mister!" Jimmy's eyes were wild already from lack of air. Monika was so hysterical that she ignored what the struggling had done, she only knew she wanted this girl away from Rod; she wanted her away from her son right now!

Mary grabbed the breathing tubes and tried to reconnect them, but with Monika hanging off of her it was impossible. "Get away from me!" Mary screamed at her, pulled back her fist and hit Monika square in the middle of her face, sending her careening across the ward and landing in a heap, out cold.

Suddenly there were nurses and corpsmen all around Jimmy's bedside, frantically reconnecting first the ventilator, then trying to get the i.v.'s and nasal back in. The feeding tube that went into Jimmy's stomach was reconnected to the straw-colored liquid on the pole. A nurse turned to Mary and shouted, "Out! Go on, get out—now!" Mary's canary-yellow top was splattered with blood from the gouges in her own neck, and she forced herself away as she saw Michael kneeling by his wife, holding pressure to his wife's bleeding, broken nose with his handkerchief. She had just come to and was still hissing at Mary. She'll be all right, Mary figured. What a nut.

Mary walked down the hall to the ladies' room and tried to clean up. She dabbed at the nail marks on her throat with a wet paper towel and tried to do something about the spots all over her top. She went back out into the hall to wait for news on Jimmy's condition. She was ecstatic at finding Jimmy—yet worried that the scuffle may have caused him a big setback. It was only a few moments but it seemed like she'd been waiting an hour before anyone came out.

First, out came the Nelson's. Monika was still holding her husbands blood-soaked handkerchief to her nose. She still managed to berate Mary despite her condition. "You will be hearing from our attorney, young woman. I'd advise that you call your own very soon. I don't know who the hell you are or what you want, but I've given the nurses strict orders not to let you near my son."

"But you can't do that," Mary replied. "He's not your son—I mean, he's my husband—if you'll just let me explain—"

Michael Nelson gave Mary a puzzled look, but kept moving his wife toward the elevator. "Your what? Miss, that boy in there is our son. Rodney Nelson, didn't you see the name on the bed? What's wrong with you?"

"No, it's not Rodney Nelson, I'm sorry, but there's been a mistake—"

"You're a crazy woman!" Monika screeched as her husband forced her onto the elevator. "You keep the hell away from my son or I'll kill you with my own two hands!"

Chapter 16

After the phone call, Mary drew in a large breath and exhaled. She'd gotten a call to a meeting in Admiral Rivero's office. She knew that it was going to be a major confrontation over what'd happened the day before. Especially when his assistant let it slip that the Nelsons were also going to be there.

She was the last one to arrive. The Admiral, the chaplain, the Nursing Supervisor from the hospital and the Nelsons, along with their lawyer, were seated as she was led into the room, feeling like a lamb before the slaughter.

"Ah, Mrs. Gallant." The Admiral stood to shake her hand and showed her to a seat next to the fidgety, perspiratory chaplain. Mary and Monika exchanged glares. "We were just about to get started, glad you could come." He had a seat behind his huge dark desk and motioned for the nurse to speak. "I'd like to begin by having a report on the patient's condition as it stands today," he said.

The large, stout woman was dressed in her khaki dress uniform and bore the insignia of a Commander on her shoulder. She opened a dull silver chart that rested on her lap. "The patient has suffered a slight deterioration in his condition since yesterday's incident." She paused to glower at Mary and Monika. "Intravenous tubes were carelessly wrenched from his veins, including an important arterial line that took his attending physician a good deal of time to replace. Thankfully, his feeding tube was only disconnected from its source, making surgery to re-insert it into his stomach unnecessary. The most dangerous event occurred when his respirator was disconnected for a period of time. Due to the swift action of our nursing staff, it was re-connected within 2 to 3 minutes, but during that time the patient suffered from air hunger which left him physically and mentally traumatized. The real concern from this is that, during the skirmish, his vital signs dropped and he could have easily slipped into cardiac arrest as he did only two days ago. If we would have had to resuscitate him again, we might very well have lost him."

Mary pushed herself to the edge of her seat. "What? But he's stable now, right?"

Her question was met with a cold glare. "His condition is stable but critical. You two women nearly killed him yesterday. With all the damage you did do, it's amazing to me that you didn't dislodge or damage any of his 26 skin grafts."

"Oh my God, he has 26 skin grafts?" Mary asked.

"Yes, now may I continue please?" the nurse said tersely. Mary nodded.

The nurse glanced down at the chart and back at the Admiral again. "Doctor Murdock examined him 30 minutes after your little altercation, replaced the arterial line, and confirmed that the feeding tube was still patent." She looked again at Mary and Monika. "It's the opinion, however, of both Doctor Murdock and myself that the patient needs to be off limits to any visitors until he's had time to fully recover from the setback, as well as for the legalities of this situation to be resolved."

Mary jumped to her feet before Monika had a chance to. "Not see him? I'm his wife, dammit. I've been jumping hoops and dodging your stupid Navy rules for months now to try to find him! He needs me more now than he ever, you've got to understand that. There is no damn way

I'm going to leave him all alone now that I've finally found him!"

"Rubbish," Monika snorted. "This crazed girl has no business being around my son. I'll not have her anywhere near him." She sneered at Mary as she elbowed her attorney in the ribs. "Tell them, Howard."

He produced from his briefcase a document and handed it to the Admiral. "A temporary restraining order to keep this woman away from Rodney Nelson. You, madam, are jeopardizing the safety of this couple's dear son and putting a critically-injured patient at risk."

He looked it all over carefully and flipped the page, noting the signatures. "I'm afraid this is all very legal and binding, Mrs. Gallant," the Admiral replied. "There are times when civilian authorities, call it gray areas, can supersede even the Navy's opinion.

"But not see my husband? That's impossible—" Mary was desperate. Her head throbbed. She fought back tears. Her body shook as she tried to stay collected. "We were married just before the Forrestal went to sea. Please. You have to help me. I can't take any more…"

The Admiral stood, raising his palms to quiet the woman. "Look, Mrs. Gallant, it's out of my hands. You're going to have to go home and be patient until this matter is investigated further. Mr. and Mrs. Nelson, I've already explained to you the extenuating circumstances here of the identification issue and why Mrs. Gallant has been reacting the way she has." The hell I care, Monika thought. "We, the Navy, regret what has or hasn't happened here, but I must agree with Doctor Murdock and Nurse Barberry's recommendations. You will refrain from any visits, all of you, until you hear from us. We're already a few weeks into our investigation of this matter and—"

"And you don't know a damned thing yet, do you?" Mary grumbled under her breath.

The engorged veins in Monika's temples displayed her fury and she pointed a long finger at the officer. "You're as nuts as she is if you think that I'm going to stay away from my son while you Navy idiots play detective!"

"Counselor, please advise your client that this facility is a military entity and that in a Navy matter, we can restrict her in any way we choose. I've tried to be patient with you two women, and I sympathize with your frustration, but you both are really beginning to piss me off." It was the first time Mary'd heard him talk like a regular person.

"He's right, Monika," the lawyer said, nodding.

"Just how long do you expect it might be before we can see our son?" Mike Nelson asked. The Admiral motioned for the nurse to answer.

"Legal problems aside, Doctor Murdock has ordered that no one can visit the patient for two weeks, and after that, contingent on his continued stable condition, we can talk about accepting visitors again."

"There you have it," said Admiral Rivero. "Are there any other questions?"

"No," replied Mary. "Just a few things I'd like to call you and this whole stinking situation."

Monika stood to leave. "That, young lady, is the only thing that we agree on." She pulled her wrap over her shoulders and ordered her husband and lawyer out of the room with her.

The next two weeks felt like two years to Mary. However, she acquiesced to the no-visiting rule and stayed away from the hospital. This was very difficult to do, but it was far better than when she thought she buried Jimmy.

Margie stopped by her apartment often on her way to her nightly AA meetings, trying to make conversation with her and encourage her. She was actually blossoming herself in her new role as a responsible, supportive non-alcoholic parent. Now that she finally knew that Mary had been right all along, it was easier for her to be the supportive parent her daughter needed. "Now, Mary. You know it's just a matter of time now before they get this whole thing straightened out. And as he gets better, Jimmy'll be able to communicate better and tell them who he really is. I gotta hand it to ya, kiddo. You really didn't give up, not ever. This whole mess has been the craziest thing. But it's gonna get straightened out, and then you and Jimmy will be back together again. It sounds like he has a long road ahead of him, but he'll have you there to walk it with him. I'm so proud of you, hon. And as soon as they let you back in to see him, I'm gonna be right there by your side. I love you, kid." The women both burst into tears and threw their arms around each other.

Mary had just returned home from an evening walk on the beach on Monday, October 27th when she got the call. The same group of people were to meet in the Admiral's office tomorrow at 8:00 a.m. Could she make it? Of course she could.

She was there at 7:30, outside his door when Admiral Rivero arrived the next day. "Well, good morning, Mrs. Gallant; you sure are an early bird this morning," he smiled.

"I didn't want to be the last one in this time," she said.

"Come on in and I'll have my secretary brew us a pot of coffee."

By 7:55, the whole entourage was assembled around the commanding officer's desk once more. The room was silent but the tension in the air was heavy. The Admiral was busily flipping through a large file and summoned his assistant into the room several times, whispering questions to him. At 8:15, he looked up from the paperwork, took a deep breath and addressed the group.

"Our investigation into the matter of the identities of the two individuals in question has come to a conclusion, and has in fact been confirmed by the patient himself."

"Oh my God, he's talking?" Monika leapt from her seat.

"Please, Mrs. Nelson, sit down. No, he's not talking, he's still not able to breathe on his own. But I'll explain it all if you'll just sit down and be quiet." Her eyes sparked with defiance but she sat back down. Who does he think he is? She thought.

"It seems that he has progressed to the point that, when questioned by the staff, he was conscious enough to write down his name on a pad of paper."

Mary sat on the edge of her seat, holding to the arms of the chair so tightly that her knuckles were white. She was sure that her heart was going to beat out of her chest. She couldn't breathe. She thought for a moment that she was going to faint. All she could see or hear was the Admiral…

Michael Nelson reached over to hold Monika's hand, but as always she pushed him away from her. All eyes were fixed on that large file that lay open on the desk.

Admiral Rivero continued, looking back into the file, now not making eye contact with anyone.

The chaplain was wiping sweat from his bald brow and wringing his hands. "Our investigation has revealed that the patient #149870523 under the name of ABM2 Rodney Nelson in the Portsmouth Naval Hospital is in fact, Aviation Machinist's Mate James P. Gallant."

"Nooooo!" Monika screamed and threw herself to the floor. She pushed her husband away as he slumped down beside her, while the commanding officer continued.

"Furthermore, it has been confirmed through dental records and identifying physical markings that the deceased victim in this case from the accident aboard the USS Forrestal is Aviation Boatswain's Mate, Rodney Nelson. The patient in Portsmouth Naval Hospital, with the identification number #149870523 was brought into a higher level of consciousness and out of his drug-induced coma to the point that he could scratch his name on a piece of paper as James P. Gallant. He also wrote a short phrase, "wife, Mary."

A collective gasp went through the room. Monika clawed at the carpet and was inconsolable. The men glanced over at Mary, who was leaning forward in her chair, covering her face with her hands as she wept, shaking. It was over. Finally over. She had a future again. She was getting Jimmy back after so many months of battling with despair and hopelessness. No matter what long rehabilitation and treatments lay ahead for Jimmy, she would be beside him every step of the way.

The Admiral handed Mary some papers and smiled, "Mrs. Gallant, the Navy sincerely regrets the unnecessary pain and suffering that it has brought upon you and your family. You are free to see your husband without any further interference from the Navy or any civilian authority. The restraining order has been rescinded."

Mary completely forgot herself and hugged both Admiral Rivero and the chaplain. "Thank you. Thank you both—you've given me back my life. I'll never forget you."

She left the building and sped home to tell her mom and to call his parents. Within the hour, Mary and her mother were by Jimmy's side, the name on the foot of the bed now reading the correct name and rank of its patient. Although there would continue to be many hours of treatment and surgical procedures ahead for Jimmy, Mrs. James Gallant finally had the same glow on her cheeks that was there the night they exchanged their vows. She looked down into the blue eyes of her beloved husband and was convinced that surely the best was yet to come.

THE END

LaVergne, TN USA
25 October 2010

202202LV00001B/134/P